Praise for

Blackberry Blue
and other fairy tales

'These joyful stories are a delight' *The Times*

'Jamila Gavin is one of our most consistently good writers of fiction for children young and old [. . .] the feel is timeless, but the stories are all original, touched with the magic of Gavin's vibrant and varied imagination' *Independent on Sunday*

'...e, sacrifice and endurance are foregrounded in these timeless-... tales, delivered in language as sharp and sweet as the ripe fruit of the title. An instant classic' *Metro*

'...vin's six stories are spooky, engaging and refreshing in their ...ality. Complemented by Richard Collingridge's atmospheric illu...ons, this lovely book deserves to become a classic' *The Bookseller*

'...utely gorgeous ... Perfect for sharing and for reading alone, ...'t recommend *Blackberry Blue* highly enough' *The Bookbag*

'A ...ing collection of mystical fairy tales, *Blackberry Blue* is packed ... picturesque moments that will bewitch readers' *Booktrust*

'...e talented Jamila Gavin is an author to watch and these ...ingly original and exciting stories are guaranteed to enchant children of every age' *Lancashire Evening Post*

'...l winner, and should be up for several literary prizes'
Books Monthly

'Beautifully told, magical, dark and mysterious in the best fairy-tale tradition ... these are exactly the stories a 21st century classroom needs'

www.

Selected works by Jamila Gavin:

BLACKBERRY BLUE

and other fairy tales

JAMILA GAVIN

Illustrated by
Richard Collingridge

Tamarind

BLACKBERRY BLUE
A TAMARIND BOOK 978 1 848 53107 9

First published in Great Britain by Tamarind Books,
an imprint of Random House Children's Publishers UK
A Penguin Random House Company

This edition published 2014

1 3 5 7 9 10 8 6 4 2

The Random House Group Limited supports the Forest Stewardship Council® (FSC®),
the leading international forest-certification organisation. Our books carrying the
FSC label are printed on FSC®-certified paper. FSC is the only forest-certification
scheme supported by the leading environmental organisations, including Greenpeace.
Our paper procurement policy can be found at www.randomhouse.co.uk/environment

Set in Adobe Caslon by Falcon Oast Graphic Art Ltd.

Interior book design by Clair Lansley at Dickidot

Tamarind Books are published by Random House Children's Publishers UK,
61–63 Uxbridge Road, London W5 5SA

www.**tamarindbooks**.co.uk
www.**randomhousechildrens**.co.uk
www.**randomhouse**.co.uk

Addresses for companies within The Random House Group Limited can be found at:
www.randomhouse.co.uk/offices.htm

THE RANDOM HOUSE GROUP Limited Reg. No. 954009

A CIP catalogue record for this book is available from the British Library.

Printed and bound by CPI Group (UK) Ltd, Croydon CR0 4YY

For Jessica, Benjamin and Stanley
J.G.

For Sawaran and Jaswinder
R.C.

CONTENTS

PREFACE

Fairy tales were my greatest passion as a child. I could never enter a wood without imagining magical characters: princes and princesses, sorcerers and demons. Even in the cities, I would suddenly see a character who, among all the teeming crowds and traffic, seemed to have stepped out of a fairy tale.

Fairy tales are often stories that have evolved over hundreds of years, and appear in many different cultures, but it is the European tradition of the Brothers Grimm and Hans Christian Andersen that I grew up with. And so many children are now 'European', even though they may have originally come from many different parts of the world. So when I decided to write my own collection, without departing from the themes of traditional European tales, I wanted to create stories which extended the European image, so that more diverse children could look at the heroes and heroines and say, 'That could be me.'

Jamila Gavin, 2013

Stolen sister, brambly babe,
A Night Princess grieves for her love.
Oddboy's fiddle, golden carp
A lost king waits: the pathfinder comes.

BLACKBERRY BLUE

Who is most likely to be happy: the king in his castle, with all his lands and wealth, or the woodcutter living in his little cottage in the forest? The Giver of Life and Death treats everyone equally, and Happiness is like a butterfly. Who knows whether it will settle on you? But although there are butterflies to bring joy, there are dark forces that watch, waiting to bring grief – like the Raven Witch and her Wolf Son, who had their eye on a certain king.

This king thought he was the happiest man alive. His queen, whom he loved so dearly, gave birth to a son. Now he had an heir to take the throne, and the whole kingdom rejoiced. The baby prince was called Just. But even before the celebrations had ended, the young queen died, and the king was heartbroken.

1

In the forests where he often went hunting lived a woodcutter and his wife. They longed for a child, but the years went by and no baby was born to them.

Some people would have said that the wood-cutter and his wife were very, very poor, but they felt rich enough and, though they yearned for a child, they accepted their fate and didn't let this sadness cloud the happiness of their lives. Every day they went into the woods to look for food: they knew all the fruits and herbs of the seasons – they ate wild garlic in the spring, apples and plums in the summer, mushrooms and hazelnuts in the autumn and, before the winter set in, blackberries.

The wife's favourite time of year was blackberry time. She knew just when to venture out with her basket. She knew just where the blackberries were fattest, juiciest and shiniest black. Everyone for miles around said that no one baked better blackberry pies than she did, and she even sold them to the royal kitchens at the castle. That autumn, she heard the kitchen gossip about how the sad king, thinking his son, Prince Just, should have a mother, was going to remarry. As the woodcutter's wife sighed and commented that happiness was a gift that even kings could not buy, somewhere on the parapets above her head,

a great black raven cawed loudly.

One fine autumn day, the woodcutter's wife drifted deeper into the woods. It was further than she usually went because, strange to say, although the brambles were thick and thorny – for it had been a warm summer with plenty of sunshine – there were very few blackberries. After many hours of foraging her basket was still only half full, and the blackberries she had collected were certainly not black, but reddish, small and hard. She couldn't possibly put them in her pies.

She sat down on a grassy bank, exhausted, realizing that she had wandered far from her usual paths, and was a little bit lost. But she wasn't afraid, because the sun was still high, and she had never been seriously lost in the forest before.

She lay back, her face upturned to the sky, wondering at the flocks of rooks that circled and cawed, and then she fell asleep.

It was a cry that woke the woodcutter's wife: a thin, plaintive, hungry cry; a sad, abandoned baby's cry. She sat up with a shiver. Everything was deathly still. All she could hear was the sharp clipped caws of the rooks, and the high-pitched squeak of bats. The baby's cry had been a dream, she reassured herself.

She scrambled to her feet, feeling wobbly and chilled to the bone. She scooped up her basket, ready to go home, when she saw a huge rambling, shambling, prickly, thorny wall of brambles, positively glistening with the fattest, juiciest black-berries she had ever seen.

The woodcutter's wife rushed forward. How could she have missed it? She began to pick as fast as she could; so fast that the thorns pricked her fingers and tore at her arms, and her blood ran into the juice. There seemed no end to the profusion of blackberries, and soon her basket was full to the brim. Her fingers were quite purple, her legs were scratched, and her skirts were all tangled in the thorns. When at last she tried to scramble out, she found that she was trapped.

She struggled this way and that in her efforts to get free, but seemed to be caught fast. She was beginning to despair when she heard a faint cry. It was the same sound which had awoken her from her dream: a thin, plaintive, hungry cry; a sad, abandoned baby's cry.

'Good heavens!' exclaimed the woman. 'What's this?' She pushed her way deeper into the thorns.

And there, right in the very middle of the

prickles and blackberries,

cradled in the briar, was a tiny little baby girl.

Her skin was as black as midnight, her lips like crushed damsons, and her tightly curled hair shone like threads of black gold. When the baby looked up into the woman's face, her eyes glistened like black-berries.

'Oh my goodness!' exclaimed the woodcutter's wife. 'You poor little thing!' And she scooped up the infant and popped her into her large apron pocket. Miraculously, the thorns didn't scratch her as she turned to find her way out, and the brambles seemed to part as she backed, unhindered, into the open. Although she looked about her and even called out, no one appeared to claim the child. 'Well, my little berry, I'll just have to take you home,' she murmured.

The woodcutter and his wife loved their foundling child, and named her Blackberry Blue.

The years went by, and Blackberry Blue grew into the most beautiful girl anyone had ever seen. The woodcutter enjoyed making wooden toys for his little daughter, and the woodcutter's wife loved plaiting her black curls, and twisting them with acorns and leaves, and Blackberry Blue grew up the happiest of children; so loved and nurtured, becoming more lovely with every day that passed.

Each year the woodcutter's wife took Blackberry Blue back to the great bramble patch where she had found her. And, as if to say thank you, the brambly bush was always covered in blackberries, which they collected till their baskets were overflowing. Then they would go home and bake blackberry pies to sell in the market and take to the palace.

Meanwhile, the sad king had indeed married again, and his second wife already had a son of her own called Wolf, who had also come to live with them in the palace. Although the new queen was certainly beautiful, the woodcutter's wife heard whispered gossip that she was a witch. Why did every room seem to grow chill when she entered it? Why did flowers die which were placed in her chamber? Why had a black raven been seen flying out of her bedroom window at night?

As for the queen's son, was there any boy so mean and cruel? He seemed to relish nothing more than causing pain – both to animals and servants. Whereas the king's own son, Prince Just, suited his name and was growing up to be noble and good, his stepson, Prince Wolf, seemed to be the opposite. Some said he was indeed a wolf, and had been seen prowling around the palace at midnight. But somehow, the king was so besotted with his new queen, he indulged the boy. Even when there were fights between Prince Just and Prince Wolf, he always supported his stepson.

* * *

The years passed, and one day Prince Just and Prince Wolf were out hunting. They passed the woodcutter's wife and her daughter on their way to sell their home-baked blackberry pies.

'I'll have one of those,'
declared Prince Wolf,
reining in his horse.

And he snatched more than one from their basket, without any please or by-your-leave, let alone a payment.

Prince Just asked if he could buy one, and held out a silver coin. When Blackberry Blue lifted up her basket for him to choose, he looked into her shining black eyes and his heart leaped for joy.

But before the prince could even ask her name, they heard the hunting horn, and were off.

'Was there ever a more handsome and noble man than Prince Just?' murmured the woodcutter's wife softly, as Blackberry Blue watched him till he had disappeared from sight.

It was midwinter when the woodcutter fell ill and died; very soon after, the woodcutter's wife also took to her deathbed. But before she died, she said to Blackberry Blue, 'Dear child, I am not your real mother, though no real mother could have loved you more than I have. I found you in the great brambly bush where we go every year, and I believe your mother's soul lies somewhere within it. So be sure to go back as we have always done. I'm certain she will help you.' Then she breathed her last.

Now Blackberry Blue was all alone, and she wept. For the first time she felt deep sorrow.

Sadly she went into the forest till she came to the great brambly bush. She sank down onto the snowy ground and cried out:

'Oh my mother, mother mine, how shall I live?'

And a voice from the brambly bush murmured softly,

'Dearest daughter, sweetest born,
Make a cloak of briar and thorn.
It will keep you safe and well
And save you from the witch's spell.'

So Blackberry Blue began to weave a cloak of brambles, and though she picked long arching canes with piercing thorns, never once was she scratched.

All through the spring and summer, Blackberry Blue mourned the woodcutter and his wife, and when autumn came round once more, she took up her basket and went back to the great brambly bush. Then her mother's voice said,

11

'Dearest daughter, daughter mine,
Go forth to the castle fine.
Bake your pies, but be aware:
The queen is cruel beyond compare.'

Blackberry Blue
filled her basket
with the juiciest blackberries and,
covering herself in her brambly cloak,
went to the castle kitchens. The chief cook gave
her a job helping the pastry cook. All through the
winter, she baked the king his favourite blackberry
pies. She soon picked up the palace gossip, and
heard how everyone feared the new queen.

They would have been even more afraid if they
had known that, in her deepest dark heart, the
queen wanted her son, Prince Wolf, to be king one
day, and that she hated Prince Just.

* * *

Now Prince Just had never forgotten the lovely maid who had sold him the blackberry pies, and he longed to see her again. But no matter how often he rode into the woods, he never came across her, even though he and his father still got their favourite blackberry pies to eat; surely she couldn't be far away.

It was nearly time for the Spring Ball, to which every girl in the land was invited, and it was hoped that both princes would find a wife. Prince Just wondered if perhaps the maid who had sold him the blackberry pie would hear of it and come.

'I wish I could go to the ball, but I'd look very silly in my brambly cloak,' whispered Blackberry Blue to her brambly mother, for ever since she had laid eyes on Prince Just, she had fallen in love with him, and longed to see him again.

'Come to me, my daughter true,
When the woods have spring flowers blue.
I will make you such a dress
Fit enough for a princess.'

Every day, Blackberry watched for the moment when snowdrops pierced the dark winter ground, when aconites burst into blossom, and wild daffodils grew in glorious clusters in the dells. But it was when the bluebells flooded the woods that she went to the brambly bush. There, laid out before her, was a dress woven with spring flowers: a skirt of bluebells, trimmed with forget-me-nots and with a bodice of daffodils; a dress fit for a ball.

She put it on. How lovely she looked, the blues and whites and yellows enhancing her blackberry-black skin, and making her eyes shine like the ripest of berries. She plaited and twined her curly black hair with creeping jennies, and fronds of fresh curling ferns. 'How do I look?' she asked.

'Dearest daughter, daughter mine,
Nowhere is there one so fine.
But before rose dawn lights the sky,
Leave or your dress of flowers will die.'

Full of joy, Blackberry Blue covered herself in the brambly cloak and returned to the castle kitchens.

All day, hour after hour, she cooked and baked, and was sent scurrying this way and that. Evening fell, and the ball started. They could hear the merry fiddlers and drummers all the way down in the kitchens. At last, the excited maids rushed off to have their moment of glory at the ball and, all alone, Blackberry Blue secretly slipped off her brambly cloak. She looked like the Queen of the Flowers: her eyes glistened, star bright.

Whereas the maids entered the ballroom by the servants' stairs, Blackberry Blue went up the great flight of stone steps and in through the front door. From the minute she entered, every head turned, from the footman to the king. Prince Just thought he had never seen anyone so beautiful, yet she looked familiar, and he immediately went to her side.

'May I have the pleasure of the next dance?' he asked with a bow.

Blackberry Blue nodded, radiant with joy.

But no sooner had he taken her hand than Prince Wolf leaped between them. 'This dance shall be mine!' he insisted, and whirled her away. And it wasn't just the first dance, but the waltz, and the minuet, and the tarantella. Every time Prince Just reached out to take her hand, he was pushed aside. In fact, as if to spite his brother, Prince Wolf danced with her all evening.

Suddenly, Blackberry Blue glanced out of the window. The night sky was becoming pale. Any moment, pink-fingered dawn would break through the crack, and her dress of flowers would wilt and die. How she had longed to dance with Prince Just, but it was no use. She must get out of the palace or be humiliated. 'I must go, I must go!' she cried, and ran from the ballroom.

Prince Wolf chased after her. 'I command you to come back!' he bellowed. But he couldn't see her any more; there was only a small figure wrapped in a tattered brambly cloak scurrying along the edge of a ditch. He tried to grab her, to ask if she'd seen anyone pass by, but his hands were pierced with thorns, and he pulled away in pain and strode angrily back to the palace.

Prince Just had rushed out too; he'd seen a shadowy figure hurrying towards the forest, leaving behind a trail of fallen petals, yellow, white and blue. He had to follow.

The trail of petals led him deep into the woods, and he remembered it was near where he had bought a blackberry pie from the woodcutter's daughter. He followed the petals further, but came to a halt by a huge brambly bush, and though he searched all around for hours, he found no trace of her.

Summer came, and there was to be another ball.

Blackberry Blue's mother made her a dress of summer flowers: roses, irises, lilies and campion.

'How beautiful you look, my darling,' sighed the brambly bush.

'But, Mother, I'm so afraid Prince Wolf will force me to dance with him, and I won't be able to dance with Prince Just, whom I love.'

And the voice in the bush replied:

'Let the seasons run their course,
Goodness will be the greater force.'

On the day of the ball,

Blackberry Blue worked in the kitchens, covered as usual by her brambly cloak. But as soon as all the other servants had finally left to peep at the celebrations, she threw it off and entered the palace by the front steps, looking as radiant as a summer's day.

As she had feared, Prince Wolf was waiting for her, and as soon as she entered, he grasped her hand,

and wouldn't let anyone else dance with her the whole night long. Prince Just watched with an aching heart. If only he could have just one dance with her and find out who she was. But once more, Blackberry Blue saw the night sky turning grey with the onset of dawn.

'I must go, I must go!' she cried, tearing herself away from Prince Wolf.

'I command you to stay!' roared Wolf, grabbing her arm.

But Prince Just challenged him. 'Let her go. How dare you insult a lady!'

With a snarl, Prince Wolf turned to face his brother, and immediately a fight broke out, which was only stopped by the king himself.

Blackberry Blue sped from the palace.

Once again, a shuffling brambly figure scuttled along the ditch as the sky turned blood-red with the rising sun.

Prince Just ran after her. There was a trail of flower petals and he followed them. As before, he reached the great brambly bush, but here the petals stopped, and there was no sign of the girl he was looking for.

Suddenly, out of the trees, a snarling grey wolf sprang upon him and tried to tear him to pieces. As the prince struggled to fend it off, a cloaked creature leaped out from the bramble patch, and a brambly cloak came down over the back of the wolf, wrapping thorny arms around it. The wolf immediately fell away, howling in pain and covered in prickles, and disappeared into the woods.

The prince lay as if dead. Desperately, Blackberry Blue tended her dear, wounded prince and her tears fell upon his face. She dabbed him with herbs and ointments, and gave him a sip of blackberry juice. Then, clasping him in her arms, she dragged him onto a nearby track, and secretly guarded him until he was discovered.

When Prince Just was found and carried back to the palace, he mumbled wildly about being saved by a brambly bush. Yet he hadn't a single mark on him, whereas Prince Wolf was seen limping around covered in scratches.

When Blackberry Blue returned to the kitchens, the castle was seething with rumours. Although Prince Just had been rescued in the woods without a scratch, he had now fallen ill and was lying in his chamber with a fever. Some people whispered that he had been poisoned by the wicked queen. Every night, the queen ordered a bowl of soup to be sent to the prince, and every morning he was a little worse.

Three months passed by, and now it was time for the Autumn Ball, but no one's heart was in it as Prince Just was still ailing.

The old king, who had watched his son getting weaker by the day, was heartbroken. 'My son, my son – who can cure my son? Is it right to be holding a ball when my son might be dying?' he asked.

But his wicked queen said, 'Of course it is. It will make him feel better. Besides, it's Prince Wolf's birthday, and Prince Just wouldn't want to spoil his celebrations, would he? And I'm hoping that my son, at least, will choose a bride for himself.'

And so the ball was arranged for a week's time.

Blackberry Blue was in the kitchen. All day she had been baking blackberry pies, and she set aside a special platter for Prince Just. A maid was about to take up the soup for the bed-ridden prince, crying, 'Oh, isn't it sad! Prince Just is dying. Is there nothing that can save him?'

Blackberry Blue said, 'Let me take the soup to him. I have baked him his favourite blackberry pies and they contain a remedy that might make him better.'

So Blackberry Blue pattered through the palace corridors and up the staircase until she reached the prince's chamber. When she entered, she found him lying there, so pale and listless, with his eyes closed, and his brow damp with fever.

She placed the tray by his bed, and whispered in his ear, 'It is I, Blackberry Blue. I work in the kitchens and I've brought you some blackberry pies. But first, dear Prince, do not drink the soup. I fear the queen poisons it. Pretend to get worse, even though you will soon get better. I have put special curative herbs in my pies, so only eat them when she has gone.' Then she hurried away.

The queen swished into the bedroom, and stood in front of Prince Just's bed, blocking his view so that he didn't see her drop something into his soup. Then she came round to the other side, and handed him the bowl. 'Come, dear boy! Drink up. We need you to get better,' she said with a smile.

'Dear Madam!' murmured the prince weakly. 'Is the window open? I feel a chill.'

When the queen went to check, the prince hastily tipped his soup into a potted plant nearby.

'My, that was quick!' she remarked when she came back to his bedside and saw, with satisfaction, the empty bowl.

The day of the third ball arrived. This time, Blackberry Blue's mother had made her a dress of autumn leaves: red, yellow, gold and purple, edged with red berries and small white winter roses. When Blackberry Blue had braided her hair with holly and ivy, she looked more beautiful than ever. She covered herself with her brambly cloak and went to the palace kitchens.

As before, she cooked and baked hour after hour, and finally, when all the maids and cooks excitedly went up to the ballroom, Blackberry Blue flung off her brambly cloak and ascended the front steps of the palace.

Every head turned when she entered the ballroom. The musicians nearly stopped playing, they were so entranced by her beauty.

Prince Wolf immediately bounded towards her and took her arm in a vice-like grip. 'So you're back, my dear,' he whispered. 'This time I shall not let you go.'

They whirled around the ballroom for dance after dance, till Blackberry Blue felt sick and dizzy. But suddenly, the music ceased abruptly mid-phrase. Everyone stopped dancing and looked in amazement, for there, at the top of the staircase, a happy, smiling king had appeared, and beside him stood Prince Just, looking fit and well. Cheers and laughter swept through the hall. How pleased they were to see their beloved prince.

'First I was saved from a wolf by a mysterious girl in the woods,' he cried. 'Then I was saved from poisoning by one of my maids, who brought me blackberry pies filled with a magical cure. She warned me not to drink my stepmother's soup.

I was too weak to open my eyes, so I never saw her face. But because of her, I am safe and well, and I have vowed only to marry the girl who saved me – and I think I know her.'

Prince Just strode across the ballroom floor, and politely bowed before his stepbrother, Prince Wolf. 'The next dance with the princess will be mine,' he said.

Prince Wolf snarled. He looked over at his mother, the queen, as if to say, 'What's this? I thought Prince Just was dying?' The queen turned green and looked at the king.

'Guards, guards! Take her away,' ordered the king, 'and her evil son too.'

'No!' The wicked queen screeched and swooped across the ballroom floor, transforming into a cawing raven. With beating wings and outstretched neck, she pecked and clawed at Prince Just as if she would rip him to pieces.

'No!' spat Prince Wolf, changing into the fierce, slavering grey wolf that had attacked Prince Just in the forest.

Everyone screamed and scattered. The dawn-grey sky turned as red as blood. Blackberry Blue's

25

beautiful dress turned to thorns. As the wolf was about to spring on Prince Just, she snatched up her brambly cloak and tossed it into the air. It floated there like a strange dark cloud; then dropped down, enveloping the pouncing wolf. With a shriek of fury, the raven queen flapped her wings and tried to fly out of the window. But Prince Just fitted an arrow to his bow and, with swift and accurate aim, loosed it; the dreadful creature plunged to the ground,

dead.

As the guards dragged away the howling wolf, Prince Just took Blackberry Blue in his arms. He looked into her glistening black, blackberry eyes. 'It was you, wasn't it, who sold me the blackberry pies, who saved me from the wolf, and who cured me?'

A soft, rosy dawn flooded through the ballroom, bathing everyone in a pink glow, and the prince asked Blackberry Blue to marry him.

'Yes, yes!' she replied joyfully.

At that moment a footman announced the arrival of a late guest. A strangely beautiful woman whose skin was as black as night, dressed in the dark purply-black of blackberries, entered the ballroom.

When Blackberry Blue looked at her, she knew that this was her brambly mother.

'Now that the wicked raven queen is dead, the spell she cast on me is broken,' said the woman. She held out her arms. 'My daughter, my daughter!'

And Blackberry Blue rushed into her mother's embrace.

Prince Just and Blackberry Blue were married after the winter was over, just before spring became summer, and she wore a dress her mother made for her of poppies, lilacs, honeysuckle and orange blossom.

She looked as beautiful as a summer's day, and everyone was as happy as happy can be, especially the king.

But Blackberry Blue never forgot the woodcutter and his wife, who had been a mother and father to her when she was growing up, and she never forgot who had taught her to make blackberry pies. Every blackberry season, she took a basket and went to pick blackberries at the brambly patch, and when, in due course, she gave birth to a daughter, she took her too.

THE PURPLE LADY

If something precious is lost, then the search must never end until it is found. But sometimes it means paying a high price to win back what has been taken away.

The last of the snow was brown and sludgy; spindly branches clawed an ice-blue sky; nameless birds crouched silently in black silhouette on naked branches, and the air was drifting with crystals. He rubbed a small circle on the steamy, grimy window through which he could observe this alien world. His search had begun.

Abu had caught the bus to the city.

'Where do you want to get off?' the bus driver had demanded.

Abu didn't know what to say. 'At the end of the line,' he replied finally, and sat at the back by himself. He noticed that whereas his fellow passengers had at first looked out greedily at the new spring-green countryside as if they would never see it again, when they reached the outskirts of the city, with its chimneys, factories and apartment blocks, its roads seething with traffic, they now slumped back wearily, as if dreading their day at work.

A head-scarved woman got on and sat next to Abu as the bus churned along a busy avenue. The pavement streamed with people bundled up in bulky coats, gloves and boots of greys and browns, like the detritus of a slow-moving muddy river.

A figure in purple caught his eye; an indeterminate blur at first – visible, then invisible among the heaving throng, rising and falling as if riding on the crest of a wave, coming closer. It could have been a mystical animal from a bestiary, for there was nothing but the swirl of a cloak of purple fur which enveloped the figure from head to foot, the face lost in the secretive depths of a hood. If anyone on the bus noticed, they didn't show it. On the contrary, they dropped their gaze; some put on dark glasses, turned their heads away from the windows, and huddled closer together as if in earnest conversation. Most of all, they held their children tight.

THE PURPLE LADY

Behind the figure, a pack of wild dogs broke up the rhythm of the crowds; grey wolf-like forms threaded their predatory way along the pavement like bodyguards and stopped in front of some tall, purple iron-wrought gates.

The figure paused, motionless, staring through the railings, its purple cloak quivering as if, like an alert animal, its fur was about to stand on end.

Abu couldn't see anything on the other side; only a swirling mist that shrouded everything, but as the bus edged forward Abu turned his head and saw a woman's hand emerge from the cloak. A thin grey hound wound about her knees like a serpent. Briefly, she tossed back her head, and he was sure he heard a thin animal-like howl. Then both woman and hound were on the other side of the locked gates, as if, like a coil of mist, they had simply slipped through the bars.

The bus moved on.

'What is that place?' Abu whispered to the woman next to him, who clutched a basket on her knees.

She bowed her head, and looked steadfastly at her bony fingers clutching her basket. 'You shouldn't ask; you shouldn't look,' she muttered. 'Don't you know what happens to anyone who catches the eye of the Purple Lady? Even to look into the eyes of her hounds is to be damned.'

'You mean these are the gates to the kingdom of the Purple Lady?'

'*Sssh!*' The woman shuddered. 'You should never take this route into town. It is a cursed place.

My daughter was kidnapped by the Purple Lady. Every week I take this bus, and hope that maybe one day I'll see her again. But I'm a coward,' she wept. 'Every time we near those dreadful gates, I dare not look. Yet I know my daughter is somewhere inside those grounds. All of us on this bus have lost someone. See? None of them is looking.'

Abu glanced around: one lady had drawn her veil across her eyes, a man buried his face in his scarf, and another held up a newspaper so that it touched his nose.

Abu felt his body go hot and cold in turn with terror and excitement. So it was true: there *was* a Purple Lady, and this was where she lived. Had he at last found the place where his sister Leyla was being held prisoner?

Leyla was one of the most loved girls in the village. Not only was she beautiful – her skin like polished bronze, her hair shining like horse chestnuts; her eyes, though deep and dark as stars in a midnight sky, could glint with gold as if full of sunshine. But it was her sweet nature that made everyone wish she was their daughter, their sister, their wife. No one had ever heard her complain, or say a nasty word to any of her friends, or ever reproach her parents. Abu was proud to be her brother, and as they were growing up, thought her the bravest and funniest and most daring of all his friends.

Leyla had a cat called Miskouri. She wasn't a glamorous cat, a pedigree cat, a valuable cat or an exotic cat; she was just a common-or-garden cat; a mixture of this, that and the other. But never was an animal more loving and loyal to her mistress than Miskouri. Wherever Leyla went, Miskouri went too; the cat followed her everywhere, waiting for her while she worked, then accompanying her back home, as if she were her most faithful guardian.

And everyone – even the animals - loved to hear Leyla singing. She sang when she milked the cows, fed the chickens or went to help in the fields. They felt that so long as her voice rang around the countryside as she went about her work on the farm, then all must be well with the world.

Everyone had heard rumours about a Purple Lady who came from the big city. They said she drove around the villages in a purple limousine with blacked-out windows, and that every time she

34

appeared a young person would vanish. But no one in Abu's village knew if these were just stories to show children that they should be wary of strangers. They warned that the Purple Lady collected the youth and souls of girls and boys so that she could stay young for ever. Worst of all, anyone who looked into her eyes lost all memory. It was true that many a person had returned to their village with their minds stripped, emptied of all memory after a fruitless search for a loved one. Yet no one had seen the lady's face and been able to describe what they saw.

Afterwards, it was said, strange, menacing birds would arrive and settle in the trees, peering down like spies at the village below. Some would strut along the street instilling such fear that people shrank away, dumbstruck, certain that these were servants of the Purple Lady, watching and reporting back. The people from Abu's village thought they were just stories . . . until it happened to them, and Leyla disappeared.

It coincided with a purple limousine being seen near the village. How often had Abu imagined it since: a rich car passing Leyla in the lane; a window wound down; a deep, soft voice asking the way; two violet eyes like whirlpools hypnotizing her, drawing her into the soft leathery interior. 'Won't you show me the way, my dear?'

Leyla was so polite, so considerate; a girl who would help anyone. Abu could almost hear her reply: 'Of course!' Then she was gone, and Miskouri was gone, seen by no one; there were not even any tyre tracks. Just the fear, the helplessness left behind in the hedgerows and lonely alleyways, in the desperate homes; in tear-soaked pillows. Soon after, a flock of rooks arrived and flew into the trees around the village, chattering their clipped *rattat-tat, rattat-tat*.

'I'm going to find her,' Abu had promised his distraught parents. The day before he left home he visited Dorcas, the oldest and wisest woman in his village. At first she warned him not to even try to find his sister: how could he possibly overcome the power of the Purple Lady? But when she saw that he wasn't going to change his mind, she told Abu that she had an even older, wiser sister called Shasti who lived in the city. 'Find her. She may be able to advise you.' And she had pressed an address into his hand. 'Stay on the bus till it reaches the end, then follow the instructions.'

One by one, everyone got off the bus. It was moving away from the city centre now, the street-lights giving way to unlit roads and alleyways. It was night when finally it reached a huge garage and stopped. 'End of the line!' cried the bus driver.

Wearily, an elderly Sikh gentleman stepped care-fully off the bus. Abu followed him. 'Can you tell me where . . . ?' But the old man had already hurried away.

Abu pulled out a torch and peered at the piece of paper with the address: *3 Faraway Alley*. He looked around for a sign, but there wasn't one – nor was there a single living soul to ask.

He jumped, startled: something furry was twining around his ankles. It was a cat. 'Oh, you gave me a fright!' He bent down, and gave a cry of astonish-ment when he saw a common-or-garden cat looking up at him with emerald eyes. 'Miskouri? Is it you?' Abu was overjoyed. He scooped her up and covered her with kisses. 'Miski! Where's Leyla? Is she here?'

Miskouri wriggled to be put down. She set off

down the road, then stopped, looked round for Abu, and moved on again. He followed, his heart bursting with hope. She turned off the road and slipped into a maze of back alleys with broken fences and paved yards cluttered with dustbins and piles of discarded goods, as though the people in this part of the city had never heard of gardens with flowers and hedges and fruit trees and ponds.

They came to a passageway so narrow that Abu could stretch out both hands and touch the walls on either side. With his way lit by only the faintest glimmer of moonlight, he followed Leyla's cat. The alley abruptly ended at a brick wall. Abu halted, filled with despair. The cat leaped up, paused on top of the wall, and looked down at him, her gleaming eyes seeming to say,

'Come on! Follow me.'

Abu looked around for an opening, then saw a faded sign on the wall: FARAWAY ALLEY. Miskouri had brought him to the address Shasti had given him. 'In for a penny, in for a pound,' he muttered, and flung his rucksack over the wall. Taking a running jump, he leaped and scrambled up to the top.

Below him was the tiniest of yards surrounded by the backs of buildings with wobbly chimney pots and broken guttering. In just one small upper window he saw a yellow light. He dropped down into the yard and scooped up his rucksack. Miskouri was waiting at the foot of a narrow flight of stone steps ascending into the building. He followed her. It was pitch dark, and he would have seen nothing were it not for Miskouri's gleaming eyes showing the way. Fumbling and stumbling, he came at last to a door. It was open; a smell of joss sticks coiled into Abu's nose. The cat slid inside, and he followed. He heard a flapping of wings, and had the impression of some kind of bird fluttering past his face. He shrank backwards, turning to run.

'Hello, Abu! So glad you found me.'

He stopped, frozen, on the threshold. A creaking, squeaking voice came out of the darkness. A low flame in a lantern was turned up to reveal the most ancient creature he had ever seen; so black that she was barely divisible from the darkness of the room. She was sitting cross-legged on a rich, patterned carpet, her long grey locks tumbling from her head like *writhing snakes.*

Miskouri sprang and coiled up into her lap, purring loudly.

'Come closer, Abu, so I can see you.'

'You know me?' he whispered.

'My sister told me you were coming.'

Abu could hardly imagine how, from one day to the next, the message had reached her. He approached slowly, still braced to run away. 'Are you Shasti?'

'Don't be scared. I'm your friend. Sit down . . .' She waved him towards an old, split leather chair with its horse-hair stuffing hanging out. 'Yes, I am Shasti.'

He moved across to the chair, but sat on the very edge, upright and tense, ready to flee. 'What's Miskouri doing here? Have you got Leyla?'

'Miskouri came to me because she knows I'm the only one who can help you to find your sister,' she murmured. 'But it won't be easy. You have heard of the Purple Lady? She wishes for eternal life; to be young for ever. So she snatches away the young and beautiful, and strips them of their essence − their youth, and their souls − and leaves their broken skeletons in the Cave of Bones.'

Abu wept to think of Leyla in such a place.

'You will have to find the cave and, from a great pile, collect every single one of your sister's bones. Then you must find the Well of Eyes, identify which are Leyla's and keep them ready to put back in her sockets. You must cross the Lake of Reflections and reassemble her on the far shore. But the lake is deadly. Beneath its surface lives the Image Snatcher. If even one bit of you is reflected on the surface, whether by sunlight or moonlight, the Image Snatcher will grab it. You will be dragged into the waters below, and that will be the end of you.'

Abu shuddered at what Shasti told him, and would have given up immediately had he not remembered his parents' grief. Only he could save his sister from the Purple Lady. 'What must I do if I manage to put all Leyla's bones together and cross the Lake of Reflections – what then?' he asked fearfully.

'You must enter the Amethyst Palace, where you will find Leyla's soul.'

'I don't know, I don't know!' It seemed a terrible task; an impossible task. Abu leaned back, suddenly overwhelmed with despair. 'And what if I see the Purple Lady? Am I not doomed? I've heard she makes people look into her eyes, then steals their minds. How will I be able to stop myself? Won't she steal me too?'

'Ah! You understand the problem,' murmured the old woman.

'What can I do?'

'I can make you blind.'

Abu shuddered at what that would mean. 'How can I find Leyla without eyes to see?' he asked despairingly.

'I can give you an ointment,' Shasti told him, 'which, once you smear on your eyelids, will make you blind for three days. The good thing is that your hearing will be as sharp as a bat's, your smell as keen as a fox's, and your touch will be as sensitive as snowflakes. But there is one mixed blessing: the ointment gives you the ability to listen in to the thoughts of all living things. You may hear good things and bad things. You know how it is with folk – they say one thing and think another.'

'Isn't that always the way in this world?' murmured Abu, and accepted the small bone box that Shasti held out to him. Inside was a strange green ointment. 'What do I pay?'

'I will want one of your eyes should you succeed in finding your sister,'

Abu couldn't deny that he felt a jolt in his stomach

at such an unexpected price. But then he thought, *One eye for the return of my sister is surely not too high a price to pay.* So he agreed, and carefully slipped the bone box into his breast pocket.

'Stay here till daybreak, then catch the bus back into the city,' said the old woman, 'and get off at the Purple Gates.'

Shasti gave Abu a draught of sweet herbal tea. His body relaxed, and he slumped back into the chair and slept.

Pale threads of dawn were already filtering through the curtains when he awoke. At some point in the night Miskouri had come and curled up on his lap. She leaped off, arched her back and stretched, as if ready for the day. It was time to go. Abu uncoiled himself from the chair, then got a shock, for Shasti was still sitting where she'd been the night before, cross-legged on her carpet. In the dawn light, she no longer looked old; she was like a young girl. Yet although her eyes were open, she didn't see him, as though she were asleep or in a trance, and did not stir when he whispered her name.

No point in waking her, thought Abu. He noticed

a large sack by the door. He knew what it was for, and shivered. Next to it lay a rope, an axe, a bundle of provisions to keep him going for three days, and a long, fine velvet lead. On the table, beneath a small silver box, was a note which read: *The sack is to collect your sister's bones and the silver box is for your sister's eyes. Miskouri will be your guide. Farewell, Abu.*

He scribbled a reply: *A million thanks. If I live, I will return to pay my debt.*

Abu wound the rope around his waist, and tucked the axe into it. Then, slinging the sack over his shoulder and putting the silver box in his other breast pocket, he slipped out of the door, back down the stone steps and, with the velvet lead in his hand, followed Miskouri over the wall.

The bus was ready to leave, its engine running. Passengers were already in their seats when Abu raced up. He slid Miskouri inside his jacket and climbed aboard.

'Where to?' asked the driver, taking his coin.

'The end of the line.' Abu was reluctant to say where he wanted to alight.

The bus set off. The passengers it collected on

the way were the same people as yesterday. There was the old Sikh, and the woman clutching the edge of her veil; the same man with his hat pulled low over his brow, reading his newspaper, and the head-scarved lady with her basket on her knee. The place next to her was empty, so Abu sat down. 'Good day, madam,' he said gently.

'You're back,' she murmured.

'As are you,' he replied.

She sighed.

They said nothing more, as the bus wound its way through the awakening city streets. The crowds, surging along to work, thickened. They were nearing the Purple Gates. The people on the bus dropped their heads and hid their eyes. Miskouri stirred beneath Abu's jacket, her body stiff with anxiety. As before, he glimpsed in the hurly-burly a flash of purple. He saw the cloaked figure moving through the crowd; he knew that within the dark hood was the face of the Purple Lady, whose eyes he must not look into. Yet already he felt bewitched.

Miskouri's claws dug into him. 'Now! Use the ointment now,' she was urging.

Abu's hand closed over the silver box of ointment in his pocket. He was overwhelmed by a desire to see the face in the hood. Miskouri's claws dug deeper; drew blood. Still staring out of the window, unable to tear his gaze away, he opened the box and, with his little finger, smeared the ointment over his eyelids. Immediately, he was pitched into darkness.

Abu grabbed his sack and got to his feet. 'I – I'll get off here,' he stammered. Never had he felt so bewildered and disorientated.

'Here?' The old woman sounded terrified.

'No, good sir – don't risk it . . .' Abu knew it was the old Sikh who spoke.

'I've got to try and find my sister. Maybe I'll find your son or daughter. Who knows.' And he groped his way down the swaying bus.

The driver looked solidly ahead. 'I don't usually stop here. This isn't the end of the line. There's another mile to go.'

'Never mind,' said Abu firmly. 'I'll get off.' The bus stopped, then immediately pulled away again with a jerk, before he had barely set foot on the ground.

Abu cursed himself, realizing that he hadn't thought of bringing a stick to guide him. He stood there, totally blind, with only his ears to guide him, and his stumbling feet to identify his path.

'Can I help you?' asked the voice of a youth.

Abu was shocked. He hadn't heard a sound to indicate that anyone was approaching. But just as Shasti had promised, Abu could hear the youth's thoughts: *This boy is an easy victim. Just in from the country, no doubt with his pockets stuffed with money to spend in the big city.*

Blind though he was, Abu knew from the sound of his voice exactly where the young man stood, so he grabbed him by the collar and said, 'What do you think you're doing? Speak up before I throw you in the ditch.'

'Sorry, sorry!' stammered the youth. 'I'm new to this city, and haven't a penny to my name, so spare me a few coins, won't you? I need some boots – I was robbed of mine.'

Abu realized that this was why he hadn't heard his approach – but then he was aware of a snuffling and sniffling. 'Is that the Purple Lady coming towards us?' he asked. 'And aren't those her hounds?'

The cat leaped out of his jacket with a yowl, and was gone. 'Miskouri!' Abu cried.

'I'm off,' stammered the youth. 'I'm scared of dogs, and there's a pack of them coming this way.'

'Just stay still,' hissed Abu, holding him fast, 'and shut your eyes. Whatever you do, don't open them till I say so.'

Fierce snouts probed their clothes; noses moved over their hands, and tongues licked their faces. Abu gripped the youth's arm hard to stop him fleeing. 'Don't open your eyes,' he ordered as fiercely as he could.

Abu held his head high, his sightless eyes open. He showed no fear, and at last the creatures moved on. But he was aware of someone else standing before him. He could almost smell the evil. If this was the Purple Lady, she was a giantess. He felt her looking down at him like a looming ocean wave; he felt her breath, not on his cheek, but riffling through his hair like a malevolent wind. The youth at his side quaked with terror.

'Yah!' screamed a voice like a high-pitched gale, right into the youth's face.

His eyes flew open.

'Gotcha!' laughed the Purple Lady, and Abu felt the young man being torn out of his grasp.

There was a shriek; the traffic stopped. Abu heard a clang of iron gates, then nothing but the silence of fear: he was alone.

He stood there, chilled and paralysed. When at last he felt able to speak, he called softly, 'Miski . . . Miski . . . Miskouri! Where are you?'

Once more, the traffic rushed by like an endless, pitiless torrent. How was he to cross the road without his eyes to guide him and no stick to warn others that he was blind? Oh, where was Miskouri? He felt his courage draining away.

Then a soft voice spoke at his elbow. 'Good sir! Be so kind as to help an old woman across the road, would you?'

'With pleasure, madam!' exclaimed Abu, startled out of his dread. He didn't tell her that he was blind: *she* would be his eyes. He took her elbow firmly, and let her step into the road, hobbling through the hooting and honking cars and buses and motor-bikes.

As they crossed, he heard her thoughts: *Has he lost someone? Is he going to go through those gates?*

Perhaps this man can help me . . . Then she whispered, 'You're going to look for someone in that terrible garden, aren't you? Is it your sweetheart? Is it your sister?'

'My sister.' Abu nodded. 'I must find her.'

'All this time I've been waiting and longing for someone like you. I didn't think there was anyone brave enough. Then you come along. I would go with you – I have longed to enter those gates – but I am old; too old. Find my granddaughter, I beseech you. Her name is Asaria. Perhaps if you bring Asaria back, it will bring back her mother's mind too. She is deranged with grief. Oh help us, good sir.'

Then she was gone.

Abu suddenly heard a soft 'miaow' and felt a soft furry body coiling in and out of his legs. 'Miskouri!' He bent down and picked up the cat. 'I thought you'd left me,' he wept, suddenly filled with an inexpressible sadness.

Of course not, silly! Her cat-thoughts entered his head. *I just hate dogs.*

With outstretched hands, he moved forward, trailing his fingers along walls and railings till he touched the cold hard iron of the gates.

He had barely pushed them, when they opened silently without a squeak or a creak. He stepped inside and entered the kingdom of the Purple Lady. Behind him, the pavements had been seething with people and the streets a cacophony of traffic, but once through the gates he stepped into silence. He heard no one: no traffic, no voices, no birds; nothing. It was as though he was not only blind, but deaf too.

What kind of place was this? Abu took off his boots and threw them into his sack, so that his bare feet could make sense of the terrain. Was this earth? It felt gritty; not like the clay earth of the fields, or his garden; not like the sand by the sea, or the lime of the cliffs; more like ash from a fire or volcano. There was no scent of flowers, no rustle of leaves in the trees, no trickle of fountains.

He fell to his knees and crawled along, touching, sniffing, trying to find grass or flowers, feeling for the trunks of trees; anything that lived. But all seemed utterly barren.

'What is this place?' he whispered.

'A place of nothing,' mewed Miskouri.

'How do I know which way to go?'

'Tie the velvet cord around my neck, and I will lead you,' instructed the cat.

Gently, he did as she said, and then, with a decisive tug, she led him further into the Purple Kingdom. 'I see a line of cliffs, jagged as teeth, dropping like stone waterfalls; they are pitted with caves as dark as eyes – lots of caves.'

Abu felt his strength suddenly drain from him. He collapsed on the ground, shaking. 'How far away are they? How shall we know which is the Cave of Bones?' He longed to turn back; to give up and admit defeat. 'I can't do this!' he cried.

'I'm starving!' miaowed Miskouri.

Abu's fingers trembled as he opened up the bundle of provisions. He realized he was hungry too. Shasti had given him a bottle of water, cheese sandwiches, salad with herbs, apples and celery, and some chicken for Miskouri. They ate greedily, and as they did so, Abu felt his strength returning, and with it, his courage.

His sharp ears heard a movement; Miskouri heard it too, and her fur stood up. A bird had landed nearby. Abu heard the creature's thoughts:

This foolish youth with his cat . . . looking for a loved one, eh? The Purple Lady had better be told.

The bird watched them for a few seconds, then rose up into the sky and flew eastwards. Miskouri saw it wheel up towards the cliffs, then swoop down and vanish inside one of the caves.

'Abu, it was one of them. One of the birds that serve the Purple Lady. It will be flying to warn her. I saw it enter a cave – I think I know which one. We must be off.'

Abu felt a chill run through him. He felt as if he were being led to the edge of the world; he could fall off into a void and be lost for ever. 'How far is it to the cliffs?' he asked, piling the remainder of the provisions back into his sack.

'If we hurry, we may get there before nightfall. Abu, trust me,' pleaded Miskouri, hearing his despair.

A thunderclap shook the air, and suddenly the rain came down like an opened floodgate. There was nowhere – not even a tree – that offered any shelter. Abu scooped Miskouri up into his arms and pushed her into the dry warmth of his jacket. 'Let's wait a bit till the rain stops,' he whispered.

'No, Abu, there's no time. The bird will tell the Purple Lady about us. We must get to the cave as quickly as possible. Now put me down and hold the cord. I'll take you.'

'But you'll get so wet,' he moaned.

'Think of Leyla. She's waiting for us . . .'

So Abu put Miskouri down on the sodden ground and she led him onwards, her fur flattened to her body by the pouring rain. With head bowed, he held onto the cord and let her lead him.

Abu stumbled on through the mire; he stubbed his bare toes against boulders, and mud squelched around his feet with every step. But suddenly, the rain ceased. Miskouri stopped abruptly. He felt her anxiety quivering along the cord.

'What can you see?' he asked. 'Are we at the cave?'

'It's guarded by two of her hounds; they sit like statues on either side of the opening.'

'What shall we do?' asked Abu.

Miskouri took a long time thinking. Well, long for a cat: all of ten seconds.

'If the dogs see me, they'll chase me. But they

won't catch me. That will be your chance. While they're after me, you can enter the cave. Just walk twenty paces forward and you'll reach the opening. Untie my cord and let me lead them on a merry chase.'

'I thought you hated dogs.'

'I do, but sometimes necessity overcomes fear. Don't worry, I'll find you again when it's safe.'

Reluctantly, Abu untied the cord and felt it fall free in his hands, as Miskouri leaped away.

He heard a fearsome snarling, and Miskouri gave an equally terrifying yowl. There was a sound of scuffling, then deafening barks gradually diminished into the distance as Miskouri fled, with the dogs in hot pursuit.

Abu counted twenty paces with hands outstretched. At first he touched hard rock; then, suddenly, space. He had stepped into the chill void of a cave. There was a fierce flapping of wings as a bird rushed into his face, pecking at him. Abu whirled around, swiping at it with the sack, and heard its thoughts: *Caw! Stupid dogs! Falling for a ruse like that. I told them to go for you, but they can't help chasing the cat! Idiots! The Purple Lady will hear about this. Then you'll be for it!* And with a fearful screech the bird was gone.

Abu dropped to his hands and knees, hands outstretched; feeling, touching, identifying stones, rocks – and bones. They were everywhere. Wherever he crawled, they rattled beneath his touch. Bones, bones, bones . . . piled up all around him.

'How do I know which bones are Leyla's?' Abu wept despairingly.

'Even if I had eyes to see, how would I know which are hers?'

All at once, the cave was filled with singing. It was Leyla's voice, Leyla's song. It was as if every single one of her bones were singing, 'Here I am, here I am!'

With a cry of joy, he leaped forward, pushing into the rattling mounds, grabbing at bones and pressing them to his ear. Every bone that sang he thrust into the sack. On and on he worked, burrowing away, gradually finding every piece of her: legs, arms, shoulders, spine and ribs. When he found the skull, the sockets wide and empty, mouth open as it sang, Abu shouted for joy. 'Oh Leyla!'

There were just a few more bones to find. On and on he searched, listening and identifying his beloved sister. At last only one voice sang; one last bone to find. 'Here I am, here I am!'

Miskouri miaowed.

'Miskouri?' Abu whispered. 'Wait. I've found her.'

'We must leave now. It's night. The dogs gave up the chase after the sun went down, and they are asleep with exhaustion. But it will soon be dawn. Let's go, let's go.'

'There's still one bone left to find,' cried Abu, desperately clawing his way among the clattering pile.

'Now, Abu, leave now – or all will be lost! Put the cord around my neck. We must leave.'

Suddenly, all the bones in the cave began wailing and rattling. 'Take us too, take us too! I am Asaria . . . I am Freddy . . . I am Jasvinder . . . Please find me. Take me home!'

'I wish I could! I'm sorry! I'll try and come back,' cried Abu, attaching the cord to Miskouri and slinging the sack over his shoulder as the cat tugged him out of the cave.

Abu ran; blindly, wildly, stumbling over uneven ground, with the sack of Leyla's bones clanking against his back.

He had no idea in which direction Miskouri was pulling him; he just ran and ran, hanging onto the velvet cord. Only when there was complete silence did they finally stop.

Abu collapsed on the ground, his legs cramped, his lungs heaving fit to burst. They slept a while, but all too soon Miskouri's furry body brushed against his face and woke him.

'Get up, get up. The dogs will be searching for us, Abu. We must go,' she urged.

'Oh, this darkness, this blindness . . . if only I could see,' moaned Abu.

If he *had* been able to see, he would have noticed an ominous speck in the grey dawn sky wheeling round in great circles like a searchlight; he would have spotted, far in the distance, a tiny moving purple limousine following the track leading to the cave.

Abu sniffed and smelled water. He felt a new surge of energy. They mustn't stop. 'We must find the Well of Eyes now,' he said, clambering to his feet.

He heard the soft croak of a frog. Miskouri heard it too, and was about to spring. Even though Abu had just shared some chicken and cheese with her, a frog for breakfast would have been very tasty . . .

However, Abu tugged her back. 'No, Miski, no! Where there are frogs there is water.' On hands and knees, he groped his way towards the croaking creature. 'Dear frog. Can you help me? Where can I find the Well of Eyes?' he asked.

The fellow's a lunatic, thought the frog. *No one should ask that question. It's dangerous; and keep that cat off me.*

Miski squawked, still crouched, ready to pounce.

'If you don't answer my question, she'll have you for breakfast,' said Abu. 'She would have had you a minute ago, if it hadn't been for me.'

'You're mad to go there,' croaked the frog, bemused that this mortal seemed able to read his thoughts. 'But why should I care what happens to you? Follow the dried-up stream bed – you're almost standing on it. But remember: this is where the Purple Lady brings the eyes of her victims. If she ever saw a living creature near the well, she would destroy them. I've done my bit. I'm off.' And he hopped away.

Abu suddenly heard barking again. It was far in the distance but getting nearer.

'The dogs!' yowled Miskouri. 'The Purple Lady must be coming. They've picked up our scent. Run, Abu, run!'

Abu ran, trying to keep the smell of wet mud in his nostrils. He ran and ran, stopping once to throw himself down on the ground to sniff. It was there – earthy water, somewhere beneath his feet; reeds grew thickly, and dragonflies fluttered across his face like ghosts. 'We must be close. Can you see anything, Miski?' he asked, untying the cord. 'Go and find the well.'

He felt a stirring amongst the bones in his sack; they were singing Leyla's song. 'Hurry, Miski. We've not got much time.' The barking was closer still.

'It's here! I've found it!' miaowed Miskouri. But Abu heard her terror as she peered down into the deepest, darkest well, where daylight gleamed like an eye gazing back up from the still black water at the bottom. 'I hate water.'

At that moment, there was a thrashing through bushes, and the snarls of dogs. Miskouri yowled, and leaped onto Abu's shoulders. Then the dogs were upon him, ripping and tearing at his clothes. With one great shout – as though it were the last he would utter on this earth, Abu flung himself, Miskouri and the sack into the void of the well.

He didn't know how much time had passed when he found he was awake again. Not drowned, but awake. Not at the bottom of a well, but in a sweet-smelling meadow, with larks trilling, as if they had somehow landed in a summer field. He could smell grass and wild rose, blackthorn and may. Miskouri lay across his chest, her body throbbing against his heart like a little engine. She wasn't drowned – she who was so terrified of water. He took a deep breath and found that the air was sweet as honey. He listened and heard the sound of a blackbird whistling ecstatically somewhere close by. He stretched, his senses attuned – except that he was still blind. Miskouri's claws still penetrated his coat and dug into his flesh. 'What can you see?' he whispered.

'It's everything; everything that people have ever wanted to see: beauty, animals, fields of gold and white; orchards of rosy apples, chestnuts casting wide shadows. We could just stay here for ever,' marvelled Miskouri, leaping off his chest.

'No we can't. It's Leyla we've come to find.' Abu groped for the sack and clutched it close. 'I have to find her. This is all an illusion to defeat us. Miskouri . . .?' No answer; only silence. 'Miskouri, where are you?'

'Your little friend has left you,' said a voice so enticing, so dark; a woman's voice, replete with kindness and helpfulness. 'Come with me, dear boy. Wake up. Open your eyes and see what a lovely place you have found.'

Abu would have looked and looked if he could. 'Oh, how I wish I could see you,' he wept – so full of longing to peer into the face above him, for this was surely the voice of an angel, full of comfort and reassurance. But the ointment kept him blind.

Soft fingers prised open his eyes. 'Look at me, dear boy,' the voice enticed him, and indeed his eyelids parted, but he saw nothing.

When only blank eyeballs stared sightlessly up, the angel gave a terrible screech. The gentle fingers turned to claws. 'The stupid boy is blind!' All loving kindness was now replaced by fury, and he felt nails scratching his face like some dreadful bird. 'Well, if I can't have you, I'll just have to leave you to the Image Snatcher,' the angel screamed. 'Come!'

And Abu heard a snuffling and slavering of hounds, and he knew that it was the Purple Lady who had bent over him. He heard a car's engine roar into life – and she was gone.

'Abu!' Soft fur brushed across his face.

'Miskouri! Oh, thank goodness you're here.'

'There are eyes everywhere,' Miskouri whispered. 'I see eyes in the trunks of trees, and eyes peeping

through the
grass, and eyes
looking down from the
sky like stars, and eyes among the
pebbles on the lake shore. I see blue
eyes, green and grey eyes, flecked eyes, and all
shades of brown eyes, and eyes as black as jet. To
look into those eyes is to look into people's souls;
I see so much sadness and gladness, goodness and
badness. Oh Abu – this is a dreadfully wondrous
place.'

The bones on his back began to moan.

'Sing, Leyla, sing!' he begged. 'Tell us when we are
close to your eyes.'

The bones set up a rattling and clattering. 'Look,
look, look!' they chanted.

'Look, Miskouri!' begged Abu. 'What do you see?'

Miskouri looked. And then she saw them: eyes of dark gold – gold because the sun shone into them; gold because they looked into hers with tears of love and recognition, begging to be found; gold because each was set in the heart of a marigold.

'Bring out your silver box, Abu,' cried Miskouri joyfully. 'I've found Leyla's eyes.'

He held out the box and, with her paw, Miskouri patted the stem of the flower, and first one eye, then the second dropped into the box. 'Close the lid now, Abu.'

So he did, and returned the box to his pocket.

He knew they must keep going. Two days had nearly gone by, and there was only one day left before the ointment wore off and he regained his sight.

'Can you see a lake?' asked Abu anxiously.

Miskouri replied sullenly, 'Not more water!'

'Can you, though? Can you see a lake?'

'I see a lake through the trees beyond the next field, flat and still as a mirror, and a boat in the reeds.'

Holding onto the cord, he followed her low growling as, reluctantly, she headed towards the water. And he was fearful when he heard what she saw: 'Reflections – birds and clouds – and . . .' Miskouri hesitated. 'Faces – human; faces of young people shimmering, shivering, weeping and pleading just below the surface. On the other side, something shining – purple . . . a palace. Although there are reeds and water lilies and all kinds of long grasses, and weeping willows with leaves trailing in the water, yet I see no water fowl; no ducks or coots or herons – just their reflections.'

So this was the dreadful lake that Shasti had spoken of. The lake they must cross; the lake where the Image Snatcher dwelt. This was their final task: they must take Leyla's bones and eyes across the lake and reunite them with her soul, which was locked in the Amethyst Palace on the other side.

'Miskouri,' he called. 'Where is the boat?'

She took him to it.

'Where is the sun?'

'It has two hours left before it sets.'

Abu groaned. He had wanted to cross the lake at night when there was less chance of casting any reflection, but he didn't know if he would have enough time left to find Leyla before the ointment wore off. He would have to risk crossing when the sun was up.

Suddenly, there was a beating of wings. 'It's a swan,' murmured Miskouri, and he felt her fur stand up under his hand. 'It must be a stranger – looking for a lake on which to swim.'

'Is it flying over the water now?' asked Abu fearfully.

'Yes, yes.' Miskouri watched its grey shadow skimming the surface below.

'What's happening, Miski?' he cried desperately.

'There's a churning in the lake; a whirlpool like a huge mouth. It's getting bigger . . . It's . . .'

The beating of wings stopped; there was a terrible pause, and then a splash like a gulp. The Image Snatcher had sucked the swan down into the lake and swallowed it. That could be their fate too, if they should cast even one scrap of shadow upon the water. But they couldn't give up now. Abu knew they must cross the lake.

'Point me into the sun,' he said, 'so that I cast no shadow outside the boat.'

He tucked Miskouri under his arm, pushed the boat out from the shore and leaped in, carefully

THE PURPLE LADY

stowing Leyla's bones under the seat. He fumbled for the oars – one, two – and began to row with all his might, trusting to the warmth of the sun on his face. Horrible groans came from below the lake's surface; things scratched and banged beneath the boat, as if desperate fingers were appealing to him. If he had been able to see, Abu would have longed to lean over and look into the water. The water around him now began to heave as though a storm were churning it up. The boat pitched and tipped: some force was surely trying to upturn it and toss them into the water.

Abu continued to row with all his might. 'Can you see anything, Miskouri?' he called.

'I see a purple glow on the far shore. It must be the Amethyst Palace. That's where we must go.'

Abu steered the boat in the direction she described, and felt the sun's warmth leave his face. Miskouri howled with fright. 'I see your shadow. Your reflection is almost in the water!'

The surface churned. With a hopeless groan, Abu rested the oars and, grabbing Miskouri, pulled her and their shadows down into the bottom of the boat. 'It's no good. We must wait till nightfall.'

And suddenly he was asleep, his head resting on the sack of bones, with Miskouri curled up on his chest and the boat drifting.

It was the sound of the hull scraping the shore that woke him. It had bobbed along, all through the night, and carried them safely to land.

'Miskouri! What can you see?' asked Abu.

'We've arrived, Abu. I see the Amethyst Palace. Stay here, while I go and find where Leyla's spirit is being kept.' She sprang from the boat.

She padded into the Amethyst Palace and entered amazing chambers of icy purple; a ballroom embedded with strands of gold and droplets of diamonds; she climbed transparent staircases, but found nothing. Then she discovered a back staircase; it was a spiral, twisting so that even she, a cat, felt dizzy as she spun downwards as if drilling into the very centre of the earth.

At the bottom, she found herself in a dark glowing chamber, its walls rough and spiky as needles, then smooth like clusters of blossoms that had somehow petrified. Shades of palest pink deepened to inky purple, and there, hollowed into the very heart of the amethyst chamber, was a purple throne.

If only I could sing, thought Miskouri, *and awaken Leyla from this eternal imprisonment*. But all she could do was miaow; the long, wailing 'Wait for me!' miaow that she had so often used when accompanying her mistress.

And then, suddenly, she heard a strange cracking sound; a hammering as if a thousand crystals had been scattered across the floor. Miskouri saw, imprisoned in the raw amethyst, bodies of light; faces like reflections in a mirror. She passed one after another, trying to identify Leyla. There – ahead! A face was pressed to the glassy rock, the mouth open, the lips moving noiselessly. It was framed by shining black hair. It was Leyla. Miskouri stood on her hind legs and pawed at the rock, miaowing with all her might, begging her mistress to be brave, to be patient; telling her that her brother had come to save her. Then Miskouri leaped away, back up the spiral staircase to find Abu.

He was lying with his face pressed into the sack of bones. Miskouri pattered over and licked his hands. 'I've found her.'

Abu wouldn't look up.

'I've found her, Abu. Come – we must hurry. The Purple Lady could return any moment. Follow me with Leyla's bones. The only way we can break the spell is by reassembling her. Abu!' Miskouri scratched him fiercely.

'My eyes,' cried Abu despairingly. 'In a few hours, my sight will return. The ointment will wear off. If the Purple Lady finds me, I'm done for – Leyla too. We'll never escape.'

'Then hurry, silly boy!' cried Miskouri with exasperation. 'You must use your own powers of self-control now. You will think of nothing and no one but Leyla. And to bring him to his senses, Miskouri dug her claws into his arm, drawing blood.

'Ow!' Abu looked up.

'That's better,' she miaowed. 'Put the lead on me and I'll take you to her.' She led him up the stairs and through the chambers, then down, down, down the spiral staircase, and finally to his imprisoned sister.

'You are before your sister. Assemble her bones now, so that she can re-enter her body.'

Abu set down the sack of Leyla's bones and spread them out like pieces of a jigsaw. Bit by bit, feeling for each one, he began to assemble them. Piece by piece, seeing her outline in his mind, he laid out the twenty-four vertebrae of her spine; her ribs and neck bones; the bones of her legs and arms, ankles and wrists; her elbow joints and knees and thighs. Next he set out the five sets of finger-bones of her right hand, and then the one, two, three, four sets of fingerbones of her left. He felt everywhere for the fifth finger, but it wasn't there; even though he shook out the sack and searched again, he couldn't find it. And then he knew he wouldn't, as this was the bone he had left behind. He couldn't bear to think that even one little finger of hers was still in that dreadful cave. But now he took up her skull and placed it tenderly at the top of her spine.

Miskouri walked around her mistress, making strange guttural noises in her throat. 'Her eyes, Abu! Put in her eyes.'

Abu groped for the silver box in his pocket and took out the golden eyes. He felt for the sockets in the skull and dropped an eye into each one.

Exhausted, he rolled away from the lifeless skeleton and lay there, feeling as empty of soul and spirit as the skeleton beside him. The darkness in his eyes turned to purple. 'Miskouri! My sight is returning!'

He scrambled over to the transparent wall behind which Leyla was held. He took the axe from his belt, brought it down with all his might, and struck the wall.

The whole cave shuddered. There was the sound of splitting and splintering – like arctic ice thawing in the spring, or a glacier moving in the mountains. Abu felt a rush of air and warmth. There was a swishing sound as spirits fled from their prisons and, like a torrential river, flowed from all the openings of the cave in one long joyful current. Just one light detached itself from the flow and hovered over them. He couldn't touch it or hold it, and yet it embraced him; he breathed it and enveloped it. 'Return to us, Leyla,' he whispered, crawling over to her skeleton and lying down beside her. The purple darkness behind his eyes faded as slowly, wondrously, his sight returned.

A pile of bones no more, as if a sculptor had

moulded his clay over a human frame, his sister's body and soul were reunited. He touched her arms and smoothed her brow; her flesh was warm and alive; he took her hands, perfect apart from the one missing little finger. While Miskouri circled them, purring fit to burst, Leyla opened her dark golden-brown eyes and looked at Abu, then at Miskouri, and smiled.

But even as he raised his sister to her feet, Abu felt a chill presence. The Purple Lady had entered the chamber. 'How dare you enter my domain,' she hissed. 'You will never leave.'

Squeezing his eyes tightly shut, Abu stood up, slowly uncoiling the rope from his waist. 'Why would I wish to leave you?' he asked sweetly. He sensed the Purple Lady's defences drop for just a moment – and hurled himself forward as if to embrace her; instead, he flung the empty sack over her head and bound her tightly. He dragged her down to the lake shore, flung her into the boat and pushed it out across the lake. The boat rocked violently as the Purple Lady struggled to free herself. At last she pulled the sack off her head and stood up in the boat triumphantly.

Too late, she realized her danger: for now her reflection fell on the surface of the water. 'I see you, Purple Lady!' shouted Abu, opening his eyes.

There was a terrible churning; a black hole opened up and swallowed her shadow, dragging the Purple Lady with it, down into the deadly water. Abu heard one frightful shriek, and then she was gone for ever.

He stood there, his eyes open. *How wonderful to see again*, he thought; the world looked such a beautiful place. He returned to the mouth of the cave to find

Leyla still bathed in a purple light, cuddling Miskouri in her arms. 'Abu? Can we go home now?' she asked.

They stood on the lake shore, but something was happening. The water was draining away, and before their eyes a beautiful garden appeared, with fruit trees and banks of flowers and shrubs. A single heron soared overhead and landed where the lake had been. It paused for a moment, then flapped its wings and flew away again, its shadow passing safely over the land below. The spell was broken.

'We can walk across,' said Abu.

So they followed a winding path edged with wild grasses, fruit trees and beds of flowers, and Miskouri leaped and chased her own shadow until, ahead of them, they saw the Purple Gates. They were wide open, and bouncing along the track before them was the bus, with the passengers Abu had met when he first came to the city – the woman in the headscarf, the Sikh, the man reading his newspaper – and also the old woman he had helped across the road, leading her daughter by the hand. This time, they didn't hide their eyes, but waved and smiled as the bus headed towards the Cave of Bones. Even from this distance, they saw a bright purple light filling the entrance, and eyes gleaming from trees and flowers and rock. And they could hear their loved ones singing: 'I am Jasvinder'; 'I am Freddy'; 'I am Fatima'; 'I am Emily'; 'I am Asaria' – as if all their loved ones were waiting to be reassembled and reunited with them.

Abu, Leyla and Miskouri reached the gates and stepped into the swirling throng of people on the other side. Everyone was looking at each other and smiling.

'I have returned as I promised,' said Abu.

He had put Leyla and Miskouri on the bus home to their village, and returned to Faraway Alley. He climbed the wall, and then the flight of steps that led up to Shasti's door. It was open, and he stepped inside, smelling her sticks of smoking incense and bitter marigolds. 'We have released Leyla, and broken the power of Purple Lady. Thank you, Shasti. Now take my eye, as we agreed.'

Shasti was sitting as he had left her, cross-legged in the lotus position on her carpet. 'Kneel before me, boy,' she said softly.

He did as she asked, and she pressed the palm of her hand over his left eye and murmured some words. Then she took her hand away. 'You may go now.'

Abu rose to his feet. He opened his eyes and found that his left eye was blind. He had paid the price. Yet through his one remaining eye he could see the whole glorious world in all its colours and shapes; its goodness and badness; its invention and creation. As he sat on the bus home, he saw the glory of the cosmos across the fields and woods and open skies; soon he would see the happiness too. Leyla was home.

The Golden Carp

Greed and Laziness are two of the deadliest sins because they lead to other evils, but Kindness and Generosity can bring Good Fortune.

Deep in the valley was a hidden lake. It was fed by several streams that ran down from the surrounding hills, gathering at the bottom into a cold, crystal-clear stretch of water in which the surrounding woods reflected their dark shadows, and willows trailed their branches like wet hair. Chi and his mother discovered it one day, when Chi was a young child. It was their secret. They went there often, and Chi's mother used to find special pebbles which were just right for skipping across the water, and she would chant:

JAMILA GAVIN

THE GOLDEN CARP

'East the Blue Dragon,
West the White Tiger,
North the Black Tortoise,
South the Gold Fish.'

Then they would spin their stones and see which ones skipped the most times.

Chi grew into a handsome lad, with golden skin and shining black hair, and eyes like almonds. He lived with his father and mother on the edge of a town. His father was a much-admired stone carver: he carved not only limestone and granite for big houses, but semi-precious stones, some of which he set into necklaces and bracelets; others he transformed into animals, birds and fish. Many a mantelpiece displayed a leaping deer, or a darting swallow.

Sometimes Chi's mother helped him, when she wasn't looking after the smallholding attached to their house, rearing pigs and sheep and cows. Between them, they had become quite prosperous, well-known for their kindness and for giving money to the poor, and Chi was brought up to be generous and kind as well.

Then one day came the terrible news that Chi's father had been thrown from his horse and killed.

The stone carver was buried along with one of his finest creations: a fish carved out of a piece of translucent golden jade, with rippling scales, and fins that fanned out as delicately as ferns. Everyone who had seen it said it was his finest work.

The grief-stricken widow locked herself away and left Chi to run the household and business as best he could. Of course, there were many who urged her to marry again, and for a long time she resisted. But then she thought how selfish she was being. 'My son needs a father to guide him into manhood,' she told herself. So when a certain man came courting her – a handsome and charming man, whose wife had been dead for many years, and who had a strapping boy of his own – she succumbed to his persuasive ways and agreed to marry him.

If only she'd known that he was really cruel and greedy and only interested in her money. If only she'd known that his son, Lu, was a lazy bully, and no less greedy than his father . . .

No sooner had she married him than he and his son began to spend and spend. They liked nothing better than to strut around like lords, and drive fine carriages, and throw parties for their feckless friends. They weren't interested in doing any work, and the money soon began to run out. No longer did the poor receive any charity; no longer was Chi's mother allowed into the town to visit the sick and give friendship to the needy, but was kept virtually a prisoner in her own house. And people whispered sadly at how things had changed for the worse.

Finally, her new husband had to dismiss the cook, the maids and the farm hands, and forced his wife into the kitchen to scrub and clean and cook and sew and fetch and carry. As for Chi, he was treated like a slave: he worked on the farm, raking, digging and mucking out. He laboured from dawn till dusk, doing the work of ten men, while Lu did nothing but lie in bed till noon, then hang around the town with his friends.

Chi was horrified to see how his mother was treated. But every time he tried to defend her, the stepfather and his bullying son thrashed him. 'You thought all this would be yours one day,' they jeered, 'but we are the owners now. The house is ours, the farm is ours. Now get on with your work.'

Day by day, Chi had to watch his beautiful mother become worn and exhausted, and her once glorious raven-black hair turn grey.

Among his many jobs, Chi had to tend to the pigs, which his stepfather and brother thought the filthiest job in the world. But Chi had been looking after them ever since he had reached the height of their ears, when his mother had put a stick in his hand and told him, 'One day, this farm will be yours, so you must learn to manage everything, starting with the pigs.'

Mother and son now lived in misery, but every day before he set out with the pigs he would whisper, 'Be brave, Mother. Something will happen to end this injustice.'

Each morning, he would drive his herd down to

the secret lake; each evening, before sundown, he would bring them home again. How he loved that solitary place, remembering how happy things used to be. Here, while his pigs snuffled around in the undergrowth, Chi felt free to wander along the shore collecting pebbles to skip as he tried to break his record. He chanted the rhyme his mother had once taught him as he whirled round and spun his stone:

'East the Blue Dragon
West the White Tiger
North the Black Tortoise
South the Gold Fish.'

One . . . two . . . three . . . four . . . sometimes five skips, and then he would cheer. Chi observed the different patterns the wind made on the lake, or watched the water fowl scuttling in and out of the reeds with their hooting, pipping and cheeping sounds, and it took his mind off his predicament.

JAMILA GAVIN

Sometimes he would hear a strangely beautiful
voice singing on the far shore; once he thought he
saw a beautiful maiden,
dancing gracefully,
dipping
and twirling.

Or was she a dream? Chi was never sure, but it gave him the courage to go home and face the cruelty of his stepfather and stepbrother.

Then one day, when the lake was as still as a lady's hand mirror, perfect for pebble-skipping, Chi spotted a stone that was just right. He rubbed off the sand against his trousers and positioned himself on the shore, ready to send his stone spinning across the water.

He twisted round for extra power, drew back his arm and hurled the stone with all his might. It skipped . . . three, four, five, six, seven, eight . . . 'Nine!' he yelled in triumph, and for a moment his sadness was forgotten. 'Nine skips. Just wait till I tell everyone!' But he realized there was no one to tell.

Then he saw something extraordinary: a vast shape loomed beneath the water. A giant fish, with green scales edged in gold and a gleaming pearl-white belly, swam towards him. Chi backed away, terrified of its gaping mouth and the menacing feelers that dangled on either side of its jaws. It was the biggest carp he'd ever seen. It came so close that its belly brushed the sandy bottom. It looked up at him through the clear water, with green eyes that seemed strangely familiar, as if Chi recognized the soul that stared out of them. A century could have passed, or just an instant; then a pebble slid out of the fish's mouth and began to sink in a slow, wavering descent. The carp flicked its tail and, without even breaking the surface, dived into the depths and was lost from sight.

As swift as a serpent, Chi plunged his hand into the water and grasped the stone before it could settle into the soft mud. He studied it lying there on his palm, and was amazed. Although it was the perfect size and shape for skipping, he knew that this was no ordinary stone. It was a creamy green, yet translucent, with a golden glow.

And then he heard the singing.

The sun was setting and its rays scattered across the water like sparkling diamonds. He shaded his eyes – and there she was again: the beautiful maiden. She wore a long, creamy silken gown, with her hands covered by floating sleeves, and her long, unpinned black hair wafting around her like evening shadows. She danced a slow, graceful dance, and sang into the wind; a song that brought tears to Chi's eyes and an ache to his heart.

She stopped still at the sight of him and raised an arm. Was she waving at *him*? Chi looked around. He was all alone, so he shyly waved back and shouted joyfully, 'I skipped a pebble nine times!' He was sure she gave a smile before turning away and disappearing among the birch trees.

Chi felt a burst of happiness. The maiden was real. He stowed the precious stone away in his pocket and hurried home, herding the pigs before him as the sun went down. If only he could have shown it to his father, he thought.

His mother was at the door when he arrived, and Chi immediately pulled the stone from his pocket. 'Look what I found!' he exclaimed.

At that very moment, his stepfather passed by and saw it. How Chi wished he'd been more careful and kept his mouth shut. 'Where did you get that?' his stepfather demanded, snatching the stone out of his hand. And Chi told him that he had found it by the lake.

His stepfather knew immediately that this was a rare piece of jade and very valuable. 'Hmmm, I'll keep this.'

'No!' protested Chi. 'It's mine.'

But his stepfather just boxed his ears and told him that he owned nothing now.

'Give the boy back his stone,' begged his mother, seeing her son's stricken face.

'Foolish woman that you are,' her husband shouted. 'You of all people can tell a piece of jade from a common stone. We can sell this for a lot of money. Now go and do something useful, like sweeping out the fireplace.'

The mother opened her mouth as if to argue, but Chi caught her eye and begged her to stay silent, so she went away to do her husband's bidding.

The next day, Chi took his pigs back to the secret lake. He scoured the shore looking for another stone that could skim as yesterday's had. He saw the perfect pebble lying at his feet and, with a quick thrust of his arm, sent it flying across the lake. It skipped . . .

six . . . seven . . . eight . . . nine . . . ten . . . '*Eleven!*'

Chi shouted triumphantly to the sky and the woods and the lake. 'Did you see that? I made my stone skip eleven times!'

THE GOLDEN CARP

And there it was again: the giant carp, swimming towards him.

Instead of being afraid, Chi now ran down to the water's edge and caught the piece of jade that slipped out of its jaws. This stone was bigger than the first one. But this time, as he took it in his hand, he looked deep into the eyes of the fish. How strange he felt: as if he were looking into his father's eyes; as if his father's spirit were gazing back at him with love . . . And he remembered the beautiful golden carp they had buried with his body. How grief-stricken he would be if he knew what cruelty Chi and his mother were enduring.

Across the lake came the sound of a maiden singing. Chi looked hopefully at the far shore, but it was empty except for a heron, still as a statue, standing on one leg in the water.

'Well,' mocked his stepfather when he got home, 'did you find any more jade on the shore?'

Chi had never lied, but he longed to keep this piece of jade. Perhaps it would help him and his mother to escape. So he lowered his eyes and didn't answer. Disbelieving, his stepfather stripped off his clothes and searched his pockets till he found the green stone. He shouted, and whipped the boy till he bled. 'So, you were lying to me, were you? Where did you find this jade?'

'On – on the lake shore,' stammered Chi.

'What lake shore? There isn't a lake around here!' yelled the stepfather.

'He must mean the village pond,' jeered Lu.

But now the stepfather was suspicious. Had Chi found a secret hoard of gems? He ordered his son to follow him secretly.

The following day, Chi set off with his pigs, unaware of Lu creeping along behind him. He took the steep path down through the woods, down, down to the lake at the bottom of the deep valley.

When he got to the water's edge, Chi wondered if he would see the golden carp, or the beautiful maiden singing and dancing on the far shore. While the pigs foraged about, he skimmed pebbles and managed five skips, then seven, not realizing that Lu was hiding behind a large boulder watching him.

His stepbrother was just about to lose patience when he heard Chi give a shout of triumph as his stone skipped fifteen times across the water . . .

And there, swimming towards him, was the huge fish.

Lu watched in amazement as the carp came right up to the shore; he saw a piece of jade slide out of its mouth into Chi's hand. Lu charged towards the water. What a fish! If only he could catch it. He flung aside an astonished Chi and tried to grab the creature.

'No!' screamed Chi. 'Don't hurt it!' He dashed into the lake, splashing and kicking to make the carp swim away.

With a cry of rage, Lu hurled himself on top of Chi. They fought desperately, thrashing about in the water, Lu now intent on prising the piece of jade out of Chi's hand, while the golden carp swam around them in circles.

Suddenly, Chi heard the sound of singing. His fingers uncurled; immediately Lu snatched the jade from him, and triumphantly made for the shore.

Chi drifted towards the middle of the lake, listening to that silver voice. Tipping his head back, he felt as if he were already in heaven; as if the lake were his comforter. He sank down, down, down.

Chi was floating, not sure if he were alive or dead.

Had he drowned? He opened his eyes again, and saw that he was in a softly wavering green place, where weeds wafted like long hair in the wind, and shoals of silver fish spun around him. Yet the song continued. He turned and looked about eagerly, hoping to see the dancing maiden from the lake shore. But instead, there before him, sitting watching, as still as a boulder, was the ugliest, loathliest creature he had ever seen.

'You're a young, fit lad,' she screeched in a shrill voice. 'Get into the wood and collect for me a sack of red apples, a sack of purple damsons and a sack of yellow plums for my winter store, and I will give you a reward.'

Chi was taken aback. What kind of place was this? he wondered. He stood up, but his feet didn't touch the ground, and he drifted gently. He seemed to be at the bottom of the lake; yet there before him was a wood, with sunlight streaming through the branches.

'Get on with it,' shrieked the crone.

'Of course,' cried Chi and, despite feeling he had nearly drowned, obeyed courteously. Without a grumble, he scooped up the sacks that lay at her feet. But when he entered the wood he saw, set in amongst all the apple, damson and plum trees, many jewels – enough to turn a poor farm boy into a prince. Emeralds hung from the trees, rubies festooned the flowering shrubs, pearls were scattered across his path. Yet Chi forced his eyes away from them and began to pick the fruit, as he had been asked. He picked and picked until his fingers were raw and his shoulders ached. And when at last the job was done, he staggered over to the crone and laid the sacks at her feet.

'Now climb on my back and I'll carry you up to your shore,' she told him.

Chi didn't think this was possible. But he did as she said. It was like being on the back of an ox, she was so strong.

Up and up they floated through the green waters . . .

* * *

Of course, Lu had got home first, not caring whether Chi were alive or dead. He gave his father the piece of jade, telling him triumphantly that he now knew Chi's secret and could get more of it.

'And where is Chi?' asked his father.

Lu shrugged. 'We had a fight; he ran away – the coward.' He didn't tell him that he had attacked Chi and left him to drown in the lake. 'But what does it matter if he doesn't come home? Good riddance!' cried the wicked boy. 'And anyway, isn't this a bigger piece of jade than anything Chi brought back?'

A cry of anguish came from Chi's mother in the kitchen.

Suddenly, the door flew open and Chi stepped inside. His skin was shining green, and his black hair dripped water from the lake which fell from him as diamonds, and his pockets, hands and neck were brimming with jewels. He began to sing:

'East the Blue Dragon,
West the White Tiger,
North the Black Tortoise,
South the Gold Fish.'

And as he sang, all kinds of glittering jewels tumbled from his mouth, scattering across the floor.

His mother ran forward with a cry of joy. 'Why, Chi, you've come home!' She threw her arms around him. But even as she did so, he seemed to dissolve away, and all that was left on the floor was a pool of green water.

Lu and his father didn't care that Chi had vanished. They were too busy scrabbling around on the floor, gathering up the precious stones, and immediately began to plan how to spend their new fortune.

But Chi's mother was desperate to find her son. That night she rose from her bed and silently left the house. She walked down through the woods to the lake in the valley. Little white flowers gleamed in the darkness as if to light her way, and a full moon hung low over the water, turning it to silver.

With a breaking heart, Chi's mother began to chant:

'East the Blue Dragon,
West the White Tiger,
North the Black Tortoise,
South the Gold Fish –
Find my son.'

Suddenly, coming towards her, its scales gleaming silver and gold swam the giant carp. She gazed into its eyes, and it was like looking into the soul of her dead husband.

'Dear one,' she sighed. 'Where is my son? Without him, what is there to live for?'

The giant carp opened its mouth, and out fell four pieces of jade – blue, white, black and golden. She thrust her hands into the wavering water to catch them as they sank. Then the fish spoke to her:

'Dearest good wife, go back home and carve these pieces of jade: the blue should be a dragon, the white a tiger, the black a tortoise, and the golden one a fish. Bring them to me, and all will be well.'

So, full of hope, Chi's mother climbed back up the hillside. She went to her husband's old workshop and immediately set about her task.

Meanwhile, day by day, her second husband and his son, Lu, used the jewels Chi had brought them to buy fine clothes and boots and belts and swords. They bought another carriage with two white horses, and held feasts for all their friends, with plenty of wine and the very best food; very soon, there was hardly any money left at all.

And it was just then that the king issued a proclamation from the palace:

'Any man who wishes to be considered as a husband for my daughter must present themselves at court in three days' time. Each suitor must bring a gift fit for the princess, and then she will make her choice.'

Lu's father thought, *If I can get more jewels like the ones Chi brought home, I'll be rich enough to offer my son as a husband to the princess. Why, I'll be as rich as the King of Xanadu.*

'You get yourself down to this lake again tomorrow,' he ordered Lu, 'and see what you can find. And take a net with you. If you can catch that golden carp, it might keep us in wealth for ever.'

So the next day Lu set off for the lake, taking a large net with him.

He was lazy at the best of times, but the wealth he now enjoyed had made him even lazier, and he grumbled at having to trek all the way down through the woods to the lake in the valley. When he got to the water's edge, he collected up some sharp stones for his catapult and, finding a rock jutting out over the water, positioned himself with his net at the ready, looking for any sign of the giant carp.

At last he saw a flash of gold beneath the surface. Quickly fitting a stone into his catapult, he took aim and let fly. The first stone, and then the second, fell short, and the fish circled just out of reach. Lu fitted a third: it seemed to hit its mark. The fish floundered in the water, and with a shout of delight, the boy took up the net and brought it down over the golden creature. He began to haul it in when, all at once, the fish twisted in the net and dived down into the depths, dragging the boy off the rock – down, down, down.

Lu hung onto the net – until, suddenly, the fish arced up out of the water like a golden bow, and freed itself; while Lu sank to the bottom, where he found before him the ugliest, loathliest old woman, sitting still as a boulder.

'Hey, you! Where am I?' he called, but all that came out of his mouth was a stream of bubbles. He stood up, yet he was floating; he seemed to be at the bottom of the lake, but there before him was a wood, with sunlight streaming down through the branches.

'Young master!' The loathly woman called out in a cackling voice. 'You look fit and strong. Go and fill these sacks for me: a sack of red apples, purple damsons and yellow plums for my winter store.'

'Go and do it yourself,' he answered back rudely. 'What do you think I am, a donkey?'

The crone looked at him with eyes like lightning. 'You will do as you're told, or you'll never go home. Get on with it,' she shrieked.

Feeling a little afraid at her words, Lu grumpily gathered up the sacks and went into the wood. What a sight met his eyes! Not only was it full of apple, damson and plum trees; emeralds hung from the branches, rubies festooned the flowering shrubs, and pearls were scattered across his path. So this was where Chi had got all his jewels! Lu ignored the fruit and the instructions the old woman had given him, and plunged greedily into the undergrowth, stuffing the sacks and his pockets with precious stones.

When at last he couldn't squeeze in one pearl more, without even looking for the ghastly creature, he began to swim up, and up, and up.

'Master!' It was the hag calling out to him. 'Give me my sacks of fruit.'

But Lu ignored her. 'Silly old woman. Pick them yourself!' he called, and he continued rising up through the water, dragging the sacks behind him and thinking how pleased and proud his father would be. He had done as well as Chi, and surely there was enough here to impress a princess.

But the sacks were heavy, and the precious stones stuffed in his pockets weighed him down, and when he surfaced, the lake suddenly looked as big as an ocean, and the shore a long way off. His body was chilled and every muscle ached. He swam more and more slowly. He clasped the sacks of jewels to his chest. Nothing would make him let go – though a white mist had now descended, and hovered over the surface so that he could no longer see the shore.

Then it seemed to him that a giant golden carp was swimming around him in great circles, and a strange figure, as gold and green and gleaming as jade – was it Chi, or a fish? – glided alongside him, and Lu felt himself being towed towards the shore.

Without even turning to thank his rescuer, he scrambled away from the lake, shivering and laughing at his lucky escape, and struggled up the hillside with the precious sacks. When he got home, bedraggled and exhausted, his father demanded, 'Well? Did you find any treasure?'

'Far more than anything Chi brought home!' he cried triumphantly, and emptied the sacks, scattering jewels across the floor. 'Surely this is a gift to impress the most royal of princesses.'

At last the day came when the princess would choose her husband. The town was full of all kinds of suitors bearing gifts: warriors and knights, merchants and bankers, adventurers and seafarers. They were not to be chosen for their wealth, but for the special and rare quality of their gifts.

Lu and his father ordered a coach of silver and gold, with four white horses. They wore clothes made of velvet and lace, and boots of the best Spanish leather, and their footmen were clad in scarlet livery. How confidently they got into their coach, with Lu holding on his lap a silver casket filled with jade, and set off for the palace. The princess's choice was to be announced at midnight.

Chi's mother watched them go, then quietly gathered together the four pieces of jade she had been carving day and night –

a blue dragon,

a white tiger,

a black tortoise

and a golden
yellow fish

– and wrapped them into a bundle.

She made her way down through the woods to the secret lake at the bottom of the valley. Far in the distance, she could hear bands playing in the castle, and fireworks arced into the sky, scattering the darkness with millions of sparks.

When she got to the shore she chanted softly:

'East the Blue Dragon,
West the White Tiger,
North the Black Tortoise,
South the Gold Fish.'

Coming towards her through the moonlit water, she saw a huge gleaming shape, with scales of silver and green, red and gold reflecting scattering sparks from the fireworks. The giant fish looked up at her, its eyes brimming with love. 'Come, wife,' it said. 'Let me carry you over the water.'

She lay across the carp's back as if on a couch, while it bore her over to the far shore. As she slid off among the reeds, she heard singing in the distance.

'Go now,' said the fish. 'Follow the path and give your jade creatures to Chi.' Then, with a whisk of its golden tail, it disappeared under the waters.

Chi's mother followed a path through a wood glinting with shining jade of every hue. She walked among the silver birch trees, carrying the animals she had carved, and found herself at the steps of the king's palace, which shone as golden as a rising sun. At the top of the steps, as if waiting for her, was Chi. Heaven itself couldn't have made her smile more joyfully, even though his skin was green from the lake, and his clothes hung from his body like weeds.

'Here is your gift for the princess,' she said, embracing his ice-cold body.

The ball was in full swing. The musicians were playing wildly, and the dancers whirled and twirled as, one by one, the suitors lined up before a royal throne with their gifts. Lu stood there confidently, with his silver casket full of jewels, while his father hovered behind him, watching with arrogant pride. He was certain that no one's gift could be better than his son's.

A trumpet sounded to announce the arrival of the princess.

She entered, and a shocked silence descended over the assembled suitors. Instead of the beautiful young princess they had all been expecting, the ugliest, loathliest creature hobbled forward and wriggled herself up onto a throne next to the king and queen.

Some suitors fled immediately, fearing that they had been tricked. Lu gasped in horror at seeing the hag from the lake. He too would have fled, but his father gripped his arm. 'What does it matter? Even if she were a serpent, you must marry her,' he hissed. 'Think of all the wealth you will have. Think of me. Go!'

Feeling his father's steely fingers prodding his

back, Lu stepped forward with his casket of jewels. He bowed before the king and queen and held out his gift for the princess. As she opened the casket, everyone heard a sizzling, like fire on ice; a bubbling like a witch's cauldron; a squelching, slurping, rumbling, tumbling, as of a landslide . . . and out flowed a torrent of mud and knobbly stones. Lu howled in horror and disbelief, and from his open mouth spewed slimy, straggling weeds, wriggling worms and leaping toads.

'Get him away!' screamed the dreadful creature, and Lu was dragged out by the palace guards, while his father fled in utter humiliation.

Suddenly, the palace doors flew open. There was a low chanting and murmuring of summer winds and lapping waters and rustling reeds.

A mother and her son entered the hall. The woman, once young, now old before her time, stood beside a youth as green as jade, dripping with lake water, his hair tangled with lotus flowers.

Chi walked towards the hag princess, holding out his bundle; his gift. Two gnarled hands received it. Bony fingers prised open the folds and revealed the jade animals: a blue dragon, a white tiger, a black tortoise and, finally, a golden fish, all made from the palest, most translucent jade, through which the sun gleamed, turning it to gold. And she began to sing:

'East the Blue Dragon,
West the White Tiger,
North the Black Tortoise,
South the Gold Fish.'

And as she sang, the ugly, wizened, loathliest of creatures was transformed into the beautiful maiden from the lake, in a long, creamy silken gown, her hands covered by floating sleeves, her long, unpinned black hair wafting around her like evening shadows.

'It's you!' sighed Chi joyfully.

Then the king spoke. 'When our daughter grew into such a beautiful maid, a wise fairy told us that only by turning her into an ugly creature would she know the true worth of any of her suitors. And only when the right man came would she transform back to her beautiful self. It seems you are that young man.'

The princess lifted up a garland of jade petals and dropped it over Chi's shoulders. 'I choose you for my husband, if you will have me.'

As Chi murmured, 'I will,' his rags fell away and jade flowed over his golden skin like fish scales.

Chi married the princess, and not only lived happily ever after with her, but rescued his family farm, which became prosperous once more. And when his mother had time, she would sit in the workshop as his father had done, and carve precious stones. Once again, the poor were provided for with all the generosity they had known when Chi's father was alive.

In due course, Chi's mother became a grandmother, and she would often wander with the little ones by the lake, and skip pebbles across the surface. Sometimes the golden carp would appear, and whenever she looked into the fish's eyes she would meet her husband's gaze, and whisper, 'Thank you, my dearest one.'

As for the stepfather and his son, they didn't return to the farm but disappeared, never to be heard of again. Perhaps they tricked another innocent widow, or perhaps they got the punishment they deserved. Who knows?

EMEKA THE PATHFINDER

Evil brings darkness and confusion, yet everyone must learn to find their own way. But if they get lost, then they might need the help of a pathfinder.

An evil sorcerer called Abiteth flew over the land and saw below him a beautiful palace surrounded by rich lands and a great hunting forest. *Just the kind of place I'd like to live in*, he thought; and, landing in the form of a large crow, he hopped over the palace walls. *With my magic powers I will take over this kingdom and make my sorceress wife queen.* With that, he transformed into a coiling, serpent-like creature that was barely human, clutching a black and gold rod.

Those who could do so fled, but not the king. Defiantly, he stayed seated on his throne with his son, Prince Florian, on one side, and his daughter, Princess Flora, on the other.

The sorcerer swooped into the throne room with his queen by his side. 'The throne is now mine,' he declared. 'Give it to me and I will spare your son and daughter.' With one wave of a long-nailed finger, he turned the few remaining guards into worms, which crawled away between the cracks in the walls.

Realizing that he had no powers to fight this evil being, and desperate to save his children, the king stepped down. 'It is yours,' he said. 'Do what you will with me, but spare my children.'

Abiteth laughed. 'I'll spare you all. Instead of killing you, I banish you into your own forest. Don't try and find your way back because I have cast the spell of confusion and jumbled up all the paths, so that no path leads anywhere. Only a pathfinder would ever be able to find his way out, and you're not likely to meet one of those.'

'You can't do this to us!' cried Prince Florian, lunging forward to strike the sorcerer.

'I can do what I like. See!' Abiteth thumped the black and gold rod on the floor. 'I will turn you into a bear, and your sister into a wolf. Now begone! And if your father is ever unfortunate enough to come across you in the forest, you will tear him to pieces.'

And with a wave of his hand, the three disappeared in a puff of smoke.

The king found himself transported deep into the tangled forest with nothing to protect him.

Each time he found a path and thought it might lead somewhere, it just straggled away into nothing, or turned full circle and brought him back to where he had started. In the distance he heard his bear son growling amongst the trees, and when night fell, he heard the long howl of a lone wolf, and knew it was his daughter.

He stumbled around, desperately looking for shelter. The howlings and growlings were nearer now. Just when he feared he would be torn to pieces by his own children, he came across a huge oak tree with a dry hollow trunk that was just wide enough for him to crawl inside, and deep enough to enable him to stretch out and sleep, safe from the wild animals.

As he lay curled up on the dry leaves, looking more like an abandoned child than a king, he fell asleep listening to the tree breathing and singing, with the sap rising and falling, and dreamed that the Green Man of the Forest bent over him. His face was old and wrinkled as the bark of the oak itself, with eyes as sharp as midnight stars, and hair and beard of holly and ivy coiled around his head and shoulders.

'Oh, pardon me,' said the king to the Green Man. 'I fear I have trespassed into your home. Forgive me.'

But the Green Man just smiled and said, 'You are welcome, your majesty. I wish I could do more to help restore your kingdom to you. But one day a pathfinder will come. When that happens, hand over these acorns. Only they can destroy Abiteth the Sorcerer and allow you to leave the forest.'

When the king awoke the next morning, he found six acorns by his side. Each nut glowed like gold, and their little cups were of emerald green.

Somehow, he suddenly felt a great peace in his soul, and knew he must just wait for a pathfinder to come.

The years went by, and on the far side of the forest a boy called Emeka was growing up happily with his mother, father and sister, Joy. The forest was their livelihood: they collected wood to sell to people who lived in the villages around, who used it to build houses and light fires. But it was such a deep dark forest, and so full of wild animals, that few people went in very far. They were afraid of the trolls and spirits who were thought to lurk within its depths, as well as the wolves and bears and wild boar.

But Emeka loved the forest. He had played in it ever since he could walk, and this is where he rescued a baby squirrel he called Kuckroo, who was never parted from him. At first, Emeka had always obeyed his parents and had never gone further into the forest than the reach of a human call. But as he grew older, he became bolder, and often, when he was supposed to be helping his father to collect logs and firewood, he and Kuckroo would disappear into the woods for hours on end, going far beyond the sound of a calling voice. He simply never heard his mother, father and sister yelling and shouting for him. When he did come home, they would give him such a telling off for causing them worry. But he would just laugh boastfully and say, 'I never get lost. I always find a path.'

Then tragedy struck. His father fell ill and died. Now, Emeka had to do everything his father had done. He went into the forest – not to explore, but to gather wood to sell in the village – and often his little sister, Joy, went too. But though they worked as hard as they could, the family became poorer and poorer.

One day, their mother married again, and in due course gave birth to a son. Although they were no longer poor, they weren't rich, and the stepfather resented having to put food into the mouths of his wife's children, so he said, 'Emeka and Joy are old enough to look after themselves now. Tell them to go out into the world and find work. We can barely afford to feed the three of us, let alone two growing children.'

'Oh, but I couldn't bear to be parted from Emeka,' cried the wife. 'Oh, my beautiful son, with his shining black eyes and glowing skin like gold buried in the dark earth, so brave and bold. And I can't live without Joy, my most precious and loyal daughter, whose laughter tinkles like bells across the universe. I couldn't bear to part with you.'

The idea was dropped for a while, but things went from bad to worse, and the children heard their mother and stepfather arguing about how to feed the family. So one night, just before dawn, Emeka woke his sister. 'Come, Joy! Let's go and seek our fortunes. Our presence here only causes disharmony. We must leave. We will go through the forest. I've heard there is a kingdom on the other side where we can look for work.'

'But, Emeka, how will we find our way?'

'Don't they call me Emeka the Pathfinder? We *will* find our way.'

They collected two apples and two slices of bread and wrapped them in a cloth bundle on the end of a stick. Emeka picked up a little wooden horse he had carved and popped it in his pocket, and Joy took a silver chain with a single glass stone that her father had given her, and put it around her neck. Then, holding hands, they crept out of the house.

Following behind, chittering and chattering, was Emeka's pet squirrel.

The moon lit up the straggly path as bright as a golden thread. It didn't dwindle away as so many paths did; even though it was thin, it meandered on and on through the undergrowth, up and down ditches and across grassy knolls. Sometimes Emeka thought he had lost it; but no – there it was, glinting ahead, almost beckoning them to follow. They walked through the night and into the next day, and Emeka said, 'We must find shelter before nightfall. We are now deep in the forest and there are wild animals here.'

Indeed, the forest had become so thick that night fell almost unnoticed, and after a while they began to hear howling and grunting in the undergrowth. But still they glimpsed the faithful red squirrel leaping along from branch to branch above their heads.

Suddenly, the path stopped. There before them was the biggest tree Emeka had ever seen. It was an ancient oak with a girth almost as wide as their own little cottage, as high as a cathedral, and with vast stretching branches embracing the space around it.

Kuckroo **darted** all the way up to the top,

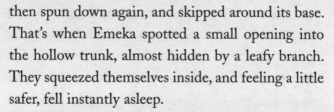

then spun down again, and skipped around its base. That's when Emeka spotted a small opening into the hollow trunk, almost hidden by a leafy branch. They squeezed themselves inside, and feeling a little safer, fell instantly asleep.

But this oak tree was the very place the king had chosen to shelter in. For years now he had been living in the forest, eating the nuts and berries, and drinking from the streams that ran nearby. Sometimes he heard a bear roaring, and thought it might be his son, Prince Florian, and he would cry into the trees, 'My son, my son! I pray you stay safe from the hunters.' And at night he heard the howl from a lone wolf, and he would weep, 'Oh my daughter, be brave. One day we will escape and break this spell.'

While Emeka and Joy were sleeping, the king returned to his hollow for the night. He made no sound of surprise at the sight of the two sleeping children, but after staring tenderly at them for a while, he curled up near the entrance of the hollow and he too went to sleep.

It was just before sunrise when Emeka awoke and sniffed a delicious smell of burning wood and fish and smoke. It brought him crawling hungrily out of the tree. He got to his feet, then stood stock still in shock. There, crouched over a little fire, was a man who looked as ancient as the oak itself, with wrinkles as plentiful as the oak bark and fingers as gnarled as the twisting roots. He was grilling fish on a spit.

The king spoke without looking round: 'How did you find your way to my tree?'

'I followed a path,' said Emeka, 'and it brought me here.'

The old man turned and said with quiet intensity, 'You followed a path? What is your name?'

'E-Emeka,' stammered the boy. 'They call me the Pathfinder.'

'A pathfinder.' The king felt a surge of hope rush through his veins. 'And this must be your sister . . .' Joy had crept out to stand next to her brother, clasping his hand. 'What are you doing in the forest?'

'We're on our way to the city to find work, as our mother and stepfather are too poor to feed us.'

The king made them sit on a fallen log, and gave them each some fish, on wooden plates that he had made himself by whittling wood. While they ate, he told them who he was and how the wicked sorcerer had captured his kingdom and turned his son and daughter into wild animals. 'Abiteth the Sorcerer has thrown a spell over the forest and confused all the paths,' he said, 'so that I can never go back to my castle. But I had a dream in which the Green Man of the Forest came to me. He told me that only a pathfinder could break the spell of the forest and release me from the power of the sorcerer. Only then will I find my way out.'

'Emeka has always found a way out of the forest,' cried Joy. 'Why not come with us?'

'I am cursed,' said the king sadly. 'The spell of confusion would soon separate us.' Then he took a little cloth bag out of his pocket, and tipped six acorns into his hand. 'The Green Man told me that if a pathfinder should come I must hand over these acorns. They have special powers: if you are a pathfinder, with these acorns you can break the spell and my kingdom will be restored to me. Will you take them?'

Emeka looked at them wonderingly. How often had he collected acorns in the woods, and even crushed them to eat when he was desperately hungry, though he had never seen any that glowed as brightly as these. He held out his hand. 'I will take them,' he said firmly.

The old king's hand trembled as he returned the acorns to the pouch and gave it to Emeka. 'Keep these safe, Emeka the Pathfinder. Somehow, when the time comes, you will know what to do. Now follow your path – and children, if you meet my son, tell him how dear he is to me.' The king's eyes were full of tears.

'We will,' promised Emeka.

'But be careful. He is a bear, so don't let him eat you up! And if you meet my daughter, tell her I love her.'

'We will,' promised Joy.

'But be careful. She is a wolf. Don't let her tear you to pieces.'

The king watched the children go on their way, with Kuckroo bounding along, sometimes in front, sometimes leaping from branch to branch above their heads. Even as they walked, the forest seemed to swallow them up and the path they followed disappeared from his sight.

Emeka and Joy walked all day.

The light was fading and shadows darkening when they saw a light gleaming through the trees.

'Could that be a house?' cried Joy. 'Perhaps they will let us sleep there for the night.'

Although the lights were flickering, and they could see food set on the table, no one answered their knock. They gently pushed the door, and it opened. The children entered, calling out, 'Anybody there?' Still no one answered, and the food on the table made them feel so hungry, they immediately sat down and began to eat.

'Who dares enter my house and eat my food?' a deep voice roared.

There in the doorway stood a bear.

Emeka thought quickly. A bear who lived like a human might be the son of a king, so he said boldly, 'Oh Bear! Are you Prince Florian, son of the king of this land? If so, then we bring a message from your father. He says how dear you are to him.'

At the sound of his human name, and the words of his father, tears began to fall down the bear's face. He lumbered forward and made the children sit down at his table and eat, and tell him everything they knew about his father, the king. Then he led them to a bedchamber and said they could sleep there for the night. But he warned them: 'Before dawn breaks, you must leave this hut, for my bear nature takes over and I may eat you up.'

It was still dark when, the next morning, Emeka woke Joy so that they could be on their way.

'How can we say thank you?' asked Joy.

'I'll leave my horse.' He took the wooden horse out of his pocket and scratched his name underneath: *Emeka the Pathfinder*. Then he set it down on the table.

As they stepped out of the cottage, a path stretched before them and the red squirrel bounded along, stopped and turned round, waiting for them to follow.

All day they walked deeper into the great wildness of the forest, yet the brambles and bushes gave way before them, and nothing blocked their path. Night was falling. They could hear the howling of wolves and the gruntings of wild animals when they came across another little hut in the forest. As before, they peeped in though the window and saw a table set with food and drink. They knocked, but nobody answered. When they pushed the door, it opened, and they went inside, calling out, 'Is there anybody there?' Still there was no answer and because they were so hungry, they sat down and began to eat.

They had nearly finished when a voice startled them. It was a high-pitched woman's voice, and she cried sternly, 'Who has entered my house and eaten my supper?'

There in the doorway stood a large grey wolf. Emeka felt the fear rise up in his stomach, and Joy whimpered fearfully at his side. 'Oh, we're so sorry. We are on our way through the forest to the kingdom on the other side, and we were so hungry. Please forgive us.'

Then they noticed the wolf's sad human eyes, and Emeka said, 'Are you Princess Flora? I have a message for you from your father.'

At the mention of her father, great tears rolled down the wolf-princess's face. 'Have you seen him? Is he well? I feared he must long ago have been consumed by the wild beasts of this forest.'

Emeka and Joy assured her that the king was well, and so was her bear brother, who had sheltered them the night before. How joyful was Wolf Flora; she begged them to go on eating and tell her everything about her father and brother. Then she saw how tired the children were and said, 'You may sleep here tonight, but be sure to be gone by dawn, when my wild wolf nature takes over and I would tear you to pieces.'

Before sunrise the next morning, Emeka woke his sister. Joy took off her chain with the glass stone and said she would leave it for the wolf princess to say thank you; then they set off again, following a path that miraculously appeared; and there was Kuckroo rubbing his paws together, waiting for them.

Nobody knew how afraid the sorcerer was of a path-finder coming one day and destroying his power.

Every morning, he sent his hawk to soar over the forest, spying on everything that was going on down below and then reporting back. It spotted the red squirrel, and immediately dived like a falling stone. But it wasn't fast enough to escape Joy's quick eye. She screamed, 'Look out!' and the squirrel vanished to safety in the undergrowth. But the hawk now saw the brother and sister.

There was a piercing screech of the bird's hunting cry as it flew back to the sorcerer. 'There are two children in the forest. They follow a path and are coming this way.'

Could this be what he had most dreaded – a pathfinder? Abiteth shuddered. 'We must prepare to welcome them to our castle,' he said.

Towering above the canopy of trees, Emeka and Joy at last saw the walls and turrets of the castle, and their path led them right up to a drawbridge and a huge iron portcullis.

How silent everything seemed. There were no watchmen at the gate, no guards on the parapets; just large ravens that hopped along the walls looking at them with glittering eyes.

'Must we enter this place?' asked Joy fearfully.

Emeka too felt a deep fear in his heart, but the acorns burned in his pocket, and he knew that only he could destroy the power of the sorcerer. 'We must go in,' he said firmly.

An enormous bell hung from a chain, but before they could ring it, the gate swung open to reveal a courtyard. A long red carpet led, like an extension of their forest path, all the way up a staircase and into a

great chamber. There, sitting
on a throne, was the
sorcerer, clutching
a black and gold rod.

Abiteth looked like a huge blob that changed
shape constantly: first like a writhing snake, then
a dark, thunderous cloud; now like a tiger, now like a
dragon; then like a man with an evil face, long,
claw-like fingernails, and glinting feline eyes that
fixed on them.

Sitting alongside him was his queen, in a swirling black satin dress all spangled with diamonds; with iron-black teeth, and lips so red, it was as though she had gorged herself on raw meat.

'What brings you to my palace?' asked the sorcerer with a voice like sizzling ice. 'How did you find your way through the forest?'

'We just followed a path,' replied Emeka.

'You followed a path . . . ?' murmured the sorcerer. 'And you never got lost?'

'We often felt lost,' said Joy, 'but Emeka always finds a path to follow.'

'Emeka always finds a way, does he?' Abiteth's voice was deadly.

'That's why he is known as Emeka the Path . . .' Emeka nudged her to be quiet, and Joy's voice trailed away miserably.

The children stood in silence. Never before had they been in the presence of such evil.

'Emeka the Pathfinder? How can a puny little boy like you be a pathfinder?' But then the sorcerer rose to his feet. 'If you are a pathfinder, you must be destroyed.' He swooped down and struck Emeka six times with his black and gold wand: once across his neck, then his right arm, his left arm, his right leg, his left; the sixth stroke pierced his heart.

With a dreadful scream, Joy fell to her knees among his severed limbs and, as she saw the light dying in her brother's eyes, he whispered, 'Take the acorns.'

Clutched in one of his hands was the little cloth pouch. Joy secretly thrust it into her pocket before she fainted away.

The sorcerer raised his black and gold wand as if to cast a spell over Joy, but the queen intervened. 'Give me the girl, Abiteth. You know how much I have longed for a daughter. Let her be mine.'

He shrugged. 'Do what you like with her.' He scooped up the six parts of Emeka's body and buried them in the forest where six paths crossed. The head he placed facing north, the feet south, and each arm stretched out, one towards the east and one towards the west. In the very centre, where the six paths met, he buried Emeka's heart. 'Which direction can you take now, Pathfinder!' Abiteth exclaimed triumphantly.

Joy awoke in the middle of the night. Never had she

felt so drowsily comfortable. She was dressed in a silken nightdress, and lay in a fabulous four-poster bed with rich drapes and a satin quilt. Then she remembered Emeka. 'My brother is dead!' Grief tore at her heart, and she rolled over and howled into her goose-feather pillow.

Hearing her sobs, the queen entered her chamber. 'Ah, my little princess,' she cooed. 'Sleep, my little daughter. Now you're mine.' She passed her hand over Joy's eyes. 'Forget everything else. You belong here now . . .' And she slid silently from the room as Joy fell into a deep sleep.

When she awoke she remembered nothing – not her home, her mother, the forest, not even Emeka. For a while, Joy thought that she was indeed the daughter of the sorcerer and his wife. Yet despite being dressed in the finest clothes and adorned with precious jewels, she insisted on having round her neck a simple cloth pouch containing six acorns, and she always left a little pile of seeds on her window ledge for the red squirrel that visited every day.

The queen cosseted her, played with her and called her 'Joy of my life'. She took her into the garden, wandering among the flowerbeds and fountains, and pushing her on the swing. In the afternoon the queen took her daily nap in the rose bower, and Joy wandered off alone, feeling a deep and unaccountable sorrow.

At the sight of the little red squirrel cocking its head at her and rubbing its paws, she felt a surge of recognition; yet her memory was still trapped behind a veil of forgetfulness.

The squirrel chattered and squeaked and sprang towards a small wooden door in the garden wall. It seemed to want her to follow.

Joy stepped forward and opened the door to find herself staring into the deep wild forest beyond.

The squirrel bounded to and fro, urging her to follow, and after a while she found herself at a place where six paths crossed. The squirrel pawed at a small mound of earth on the path leading northwards. Suddenly, she felt the pouch of acorns burning into her breast, and a voice came from beneath the earth:

> *'I am Emeka the Pathfinder –*
> *Find me.*
> *Emeka the Pathfinder –*
> *Find me.'*

Now she remembered everything. Like a thunderbolt striking her brain, Joy remembered who she was; she remembered her real mother and her little home, and the time when she was happy. And she remembered Emeka.

'Emeka, my brother!' she wept. 'And you are Kuckroo!' She watched Emeka's pet, the little red squirrel, hopping over the mound and scraping at the earth, and she too began digging frantically with

142

her hands until she had uncovered Emeka's head, which faced north. How she wailed with grief and cradled it. But now the pouch of acorns around her neck rattled as if trying to break free, and a voice seemed to be whispering,

'I am Emeka the Pathfinder . . .
I am Emeka the Pathfinder –
Plant me.'

Joy took out an acorn and placed it inside Emeka's mouth and covered his head over with earth again. Then she heard the queen calling her. 'Joy, Joy! Where are you?' And hastily, she ran back through the gate into the garden.

'Where have you been, my darling daughter?' asked the queen when she returned.

'Oh, just planting acorns in the forest. I want so much to see them grow into oaks.'

The queen laughed. 'Why, you silly little goose, oaks take hundreds of years to grow. You will never see your acorns become oaks. But off you go, if it makes you happy.' Her red mouth opened in a smile, showing her iron-black teeth.

The next day, while the queen slept, Joy followed the squirrel into the forest again. They came to the place where the six paths crossed, and the squirrel leaped onto another mound of earth along a path running to the east, and once more she heard whispering:

'I am Emeka the Pathfinder –
Find me.
Emeka the Pathfinder –
Plant me.'

She went over to where Kuckroo was scraping the earth and, as before, dug with her fingers till she had uncovered an arm. It was Emeka's right arm, its hand open and stretching towards the west. She took it up and kissed it, weeping profusely, then placed an acorn in the open hand and covered it over with earth again. Then she turned up the soil to the east and found his left arm. Kissing it tenderly, she placed the third acorn in the outstretched hand just as she heard the queen calling for her.

'Joy, Joy, where are you, my darling girl?'

144

The following day, as soon as the queen fell asleep, Joy again entered the forest. There was the squirrel, hopping over another mound of earth and pawing at the soil, and she heard the whispering:

'I am Emeka the Pathfinder –
Find me.
I am Emeka the Pathfinder –
Plant me.'

She dug into the earth and found his right leg stretching towards the south-west, and then his left leg pointing to the south-east. As before, she placed a fourth and fifth acorn between the toes of each foot. There was just one acorn left to plant, but again she had to return as the queen woke and called for her.

It was the fourth day. The queen had settled into her rosy bower for her afternoon nap, and Joy was desperate to set off for the forest so that Kuckroo could show her where she should plant her last acorn. The queen's breathing had become soft and steady as one asleep, and Joy was about to steal away when the queen's eyes flew open and she sat up reproachfully. 'Where are you going, my darling daughter?'

'Just into the forest, Mother, to plant acorns. I do so want to see them grow into oak trees.'

The queen embraced her. 'I don't yet feel sleepy. Why don't we take a walk in the forest? You can show me where you have planted these acorns of yours.'

Joy had to think quickly. She *had* to plant her last acorn.

But the queen took her arm and went towards the small wooden door in the garden wall. 'Well, where did you plant them?' she demanded.

'This way,' said Joy as they walked out into the shady forest, and she led her along a path in the opposite direction. It took them into a deeper and darker part of the forest, and soon the queen was tugging her gown free of the thicket, and giving little gasps of unease at the sounds of rustling and grunts in the undergrowth.

'Aren't we there yet?' she demanded impatiently.

'Oh dear,' sighed Joy. 'The forest is so big, and

everywhere looks the same. I can't remember which path I took and where I buried them. I'm so sorry.' And she looked as if she were about to cry.

'Come, come, my dear. I'm not surprised you can't find them in this wilderness. We'd better go back before we get lost.' And the queen hurriedly tugged Joy round and they returned to the palace walls.

It was still warm and sunny in the garden, and at last the queen yawned. 'We may not have found your acorns, my dear,' she murmured, 'but the exercise has made me sleepy.' She stretched herself out on her bed of rose petals. 'Stay with me while I sleep a little, my child – you are so beloved.'

So Joy stayed with her, though she was desperate to leave. She soothed her brow and sang a soft lullaby, feeling nothing but dread for this sorcerer's queen, with her blood-red mouth and iron-black teeth. And at last she slept.

Joy crept away and sped from the gardens into the forest to see where she should plant her sixth and last acorn. There, at the very point where the six paths crossed, was the red squirrel, pawing at a small mound of earth. The last acorn in the pouch

around her neck began to burn with such intensity
that Joy ripped it off. She scraped away the earth,
and there was Emeka's heart.

'Oh brother, Emeka,' Joy wept as she planted the
last acorn and laid his heart over it. 'Dear brother,
live!'

Then the queen's voice called to her from the
palace: 'Beloved daughter, why did you leave me?
Where are you?'

Joy fled back to the little wooden door and into
the garden. 'I'm here, I'm here!' she cried. 'I was only
trying to remember where I planted my acorns.'

That night, when the queen was preparing Joy
for bed, she exclaimed, 'Why, my darling daughter,
how came you to have such a mark on your chest?'
And, sure enough, there was a burn, the shape and
size of an acorn. 'It wasn't there before!' The queen's
eyes narrowed to slits, and her red mouth twitched
with suspicion.

'Oh, it's nothing,' laughed Joy. 'I had a slight
cough, so I pressed a hot silver spoon to my chest.
Silly me!' And giving the queen a goodnight kiss,
she slipped into bed.

But as soon as the queen had gone, Joy heard a

scratching at her
window, and there was
Kuckroo, his tail quivering
with agitation, rubbing his
paws together and giving little
jumps. Joy understood his message:
*You must leave now. Escape while
you can!*

She climbed out of the window,
and scrambled down the twisted vine
onto the grass. Bounding and twirling,
Kuckroo led Joy to the wooden door
and out into the forest. 'Run, run!'
the squirrel urged.

Meanwhile, the queen had gone
to her husband the sorcerer. 'I fear
this child cannot be my daughter
after all, the little witch. What shall
we do with her?'

When Abiteth heard that Joy
had been planting acorns in the
forest, and that she had an acorn burn
on her chest, he suddenly understood

149

and shuddered with fear. The power of the path-finder had not yet been totally destroyed.

'Bring the girl here,' he ordered.

But when the queen went to Joy's bedchamber, she saw the empty bed and the open window.

The sorcerer squawked and hissed with fury; it was the caw of the crow, the spitting of the serpent – a howl of the devil. He spread out his arms and his black flowing cloak, and quickly turned into a monstrous flying creature.

He knew his only hope was to catch Joy and destroy her.

Joy ran and ran, deep into the forest, while Abiteth called on all the wild beasts to find her and kill her. The trees swished and swirled, and acorns rained to the ground.

She came to the Wolf Princess's cottage, and burst inside, crying, 'Save me, save me!'

A snarling wolf crouched, ready to spring, with bared teeth. Joy saw the silver chain and glass stone that she had left for the princess, and snatching it up, she flung it around the wolf's neck. Immediately, the spell was broken, and there stood Princess Flora.

But the trees were rattling, and all the wild beasts were howling and roaring. 'Find the child!' screamed the sorcerer, bringing darkness to the forest with his billowing cloak.

Princess Flora grasped Joy's arm. 'We must go to my brother, the bear: he will save us.'

They came to the Bear Prince's cottage, and Flora rushed inside. When he saw her, the bear lunged forward with a shattering roar, about to eat her up. But Joy grasped Emeka's little wooden horse, which still stood on the table, and held it before him. 'This is the horse made by Emeka the Pathfinder. Save him!' she cried, and she ran outside.

In an instant, the bear turned into Prince Florian, and the little wooden horse became a noble oak-brown stallion with a mane as shiny as acorns; he pawed at the earth, eager to be off.

Florian and Flora leaped onto the horse and reached down for Joy, but the sorcerer descended like a tempest and enveloped her in an impenetrable darkness, separating her from them. All she could hear was their frantic voices fading into the distance.

The forest crackled as if on fire. 'Kill her! Kill! Kill!' Abiteth ordered the wild beasts.

Gleaming eyes stared out of the darkness, but nothing moved to attack her. 'Obey me!' shrieked the sorcerer, but suddenly, there was Kuckroo, scampering at her feet.

'Follow me, follow me!' The gleaming eyes of the beasts lit up a way through the forest till Joy came full circle, back where the six paths met; where she had planted the six acorns over Emeka's limbs. A bright moon lit up the sky.

To her amazement, she saw that the acorns she had planted had grown into six giant oaks, and from every tree ran a path, each in a different direction.

Abiteth billowed towards them like a tornado, waving his black and gold wand.

Joy sank to her knees at the very centre of the crossed paths and called out, 'Emeka!'

Out of the burial mounds came, firstly, a head from the north, then arms from the east and west, and two legs from the south, and from the very centre, pointing up to heaven, a heart. They merged together and became one body: Emeka, singing at the top of his voice, 'I am Emeka the Pathfinder!'

The branches of the six oaks reached out from all points of his body, their greenery stretching towards earth and sky, and became the

Green Man,

scattering the clouds in a burst of thunder. The sorcerer Abiteth disintegrated into thousands of hailstones, which fell to earth and melted away.

All around, more paths suddenly emerged, like prisoners coming out of the darkness of incarceration; paths that ran in all directions through the forest, taking travellers to their destinations.

'We're free, we're free! The paths are free – the travellers are free.'

Emeka and Joy flew into each other's arms, and Kuckroo leaped up onto Emeka's shoulder and nibbled his ear.

The sorcerer's queen stood on the castle wall surrounded by the ravens. She gave a great howl of grief. 'Oh Joy, how I wished you had been my child, my beloved daughter!' She raised her arms as if to wave goodbye and, with the ravens, rose into the stormy sky and flew away. And suddenly the sun shone, the birds of the forest broke into song, and everything looked golden.

A rider came out of the forest along a path from the south, mounted on Emeka's horse. It was the king, looking upright and strong, his face brimming with happiness. Holding the bridle on either side were Prince Florian and Princess Flora.

And so Emeka the Pathfinder and his sister, Joy, broke the power of the Abiteth the Sorcerer and restored a kingdom to its king and a father to his children.

The king and his children begged Joy and Emeka to stay with them for ever, and for a while they lived in great happiness. But one day, Emeka went before the king. 'Sire,' he said, bowing low. 'The time has come for me to go. I am a pathfinder, and must seek my own path of destiny.'

Joy wept to see her brother go, but her path had ended at the palace, where she and Prince Florian had fallen in love and pledged to marry.

Princess Flora also wept to see Emeka leave. How she hoped that, perhaps, his path would one day lead him back to the castle, where she would be waiting.

They all stood on the castle ramparts and watched as Emeka mounted his oak-brown horse, and set off along a path, following wherever it would take him.

ODDBOY

Is anything more important than the love of family and a home? When other things seem more valuable and each wants something that another has, jealousy and deceit bring havoc. Can there ever be redemption?

A magician saw a beggar boy in the street playing a one-stringed instrument with such skill that he stopped immediately, and conjured up a beautiful violin of shining gold, with four strings spun from spider's thread, and a bow with hair from a unicorn's tail. He said to the child, 'Do you want to try it?'

The boy couldn't resist, and as soon as the bow touched the strings, his fingers hardly seemed to be his own as they ran up and down, making the most beautiful sounds he had ever heard. He felt he *must* have it. It was as if a spell had been cast over him.

'If you come with me, I'll give you this violin,' said the magician. 'I need someone to play to me in my lonely kingdom.' And before the boy had a chance to reply, the magician whisked him away to his abode in a dark, gloomy country.

Looking in horror at a grey, barren land of mist, which seemed to have no people or animals or trees and flowers, the boy begged to go back to his home. Only now that he had left it did he realize what a wonderful land of colour, smells and sunshine he came from. But it was too late. Instead, the magician took the violin and, inside the body of the instrument, painted oranges and lemons and dark green leaves, and white snowy mountains that ran down to an azure sea. 'This will remind you of home,' he said.

Every day, the magician commanded the boy to play, and he obeyed. But every now and then, the magician would go away and he would warn the boy sternly, 'Never go down beyond the mist which encircles my kingdom, for if you do you will lose your voice.' Sometimes the boy, longing for home, would go to the very edge of the curtain of mist and listen to the sounds drifting up to him from the village far below – especially in the summer, when he heard the happy sounds of fiddlers and dancers, and families enjoying themselves on the village green; just like the sounds of home. How he yearned to join them. And he began to think, *What use is my voice if I have no one to talk to?*

One day, the magician had to go away. The boy took his violin and went down to the very edge of the curtain of mist. Sounds of music, dancing and merriment rose up the slopes, and he too began to play and jig around. When he heard the laughing voices, he laughed too, and sang along with them until night fell. Then the sounds died away as everyone went home. The boy looked up into the sky – which was no sky, but more like a shroud that bound him to this hard rocky earth. Just as by day he saw no sun, by night he saw no moon or stars; only the impenetrable grey fog becoming darker and darker. Suddenly, he knew he must escape this barren, colourless mountain, where no birds flew, where the only sound to be heard was the music of his violin. He knew he must go, whatever the cost, and burst through this mist to the other side, even if it meant losing his voice.

What a surprise when, the next morning, the villagers at the foot of the mountain awoke to find a boy standing in the middle of the market square, wearing only white cotton pyjamas, with a violin tucked under his arm. His skin was as dark as

India, his eyes as black as Africa, and his hair as tangled as unkempt brambles.

Children found him first and laughed. 'Who's that odd boy?' When he seemed unable to tell them his name, they called him Oddboy. The dogs didn't growl at him, but sniffed around his bare feet with their tails wagging. Soon a crowd gathered, and asked his name, but he shrugged and shook his head. They asked where he had come from; having no voice, he simply tucked the fiddle under his chin and began to play.

At first the notes rose from the strings like trees wailing and whistling in the wind, or birds calling to each other in the forest, and everyone stood spellbound. But then he began to tap his foot, and the music seemed to descend to earth with jig-gety-joggety rhythms, and soon other villagers appeared, still sleepy from the night before. But even so, as the boy played, they couldn't help link-ing arms, dancing and swinging in circles and squares and hops and skips. Even babies bounced up and down in their mothers' arms, and everybody smiled, then laughed, then cheered.

But a few people wanted to drive him away.

'Send him back where he came from,' one of them muttered.

'But where *did* he come from?' asked another.

Then they all looked up the mountain behind them and nodded to each other. It loomed high above the village, with its steep sides, and chasms that could swallow you up. Sheer precipices fell thousands of feet, and its peak was never seen, for there was always a barrier of white swirling mist above which no one, in living memory, had ever ventured.

'A magician lives up there,' they told each other, and warned their children never to climb too high.

A few brave ones had gone to the very edges of this white void, but never beyond, for how could anyone see the path, or know where the dangerous chasms and crevasses were? Sometimes, far above, they would hear the rumble of tumbling rocks, and the roar of landslides, and say, 'There's the magician casting his spells.'

'That's it!' laughed someone. 'The odd boy came down from the mountain!'

'Well, if he did, he should go back; he may be a sorcerer's child,' someone warned, and they all laughed a little shakily, for no one was ever sure if the stories were true.

'At any rate, Oddboy doesn't belong here,' they agreed, and they pointed him towards the mountain, telling him to go back where he'd come from.

But Oddboy had sacrificed his voice to be in a land of colour and sound and people again. Although he could say nothing, his violin spoke for him: of how he longed to stay in this pretty village with its honey stone walls, and its orchards of green apples, golden pears and red plums and cherries; and how he delighted in the bubbling river that tumbled down from some unknown mountain source above. His music danced as he thought of all this beauty around him, and people couldn't help smiling when he seemed able to express all the things they wanted to hear: happiness, thoughtfulness, jollity and, sometimes, heartbreaking sadness. He never wanted to go back to the grey kingdom of the magician. But still they wanted to send him away.

Then old blind Mr Petamenghi, the village music teacher and fiddler for all events, said, 'No, no, no! Don't talk silly nonsense. If he wants to stay, let him stay. We can't let such a wonderful fiddler go. He can live with me and my grandson, Remus. Never have I heard such magical playing in all my born days. If only . . .' He paused, then bit his lip and said nothing more.

But Remus knew that, though he had been brought up to play from the cradle and was expected to follow in his grandfather's footsteps, he would never be as good a violinist as Oddboy. All the stranger had to do was lift his fiddle under his chin and play, and people would begin to tap their feet, or sway dreamily, or break into a dance.

* * *

164

Oddboy soon earned his keep, for he was always in demand to play at weddings, funerals, bar mitzvahs, name days, birthdays, anniversaries, fêtes and parties, and he quickly began to feel at home. Every evening after supper, Mr Petamenghi would sit in his chair by the fire and say, 'Oddboy, play for me,' and Oddboy would pick up his fiddle and play a tune which seemed full of mysterious longing, but which always expressed all his gratitude.

'What is the name of that melody?' asked Grandfather Petamenghi. And when Oddboy couldn't reply, he said, 'Well, it seems to me to sing of a land of colour and sunshine. Is that where you came from? Is that where your home is? I'll call your tune "The Song of Home",' and he muttered words which somehow came into his head, and which fitted:

'I sing of a land
Where roses blow,
And lemons grow,
And orange trees float in a deep green shade.'

How it soothed the blind old man, the beautiful

sounds bringing him greater joy and peace than he had ever known.

How galling for Remus, who had to carry on caring for his grandfather, as he had done for years: cooking and cleaning, fetching and carrying, and then practising the violin as much as he could, because it meant so much to Grandfather, who wanted him to be the village fiddler when he himself was too old to carry on.

Yet, even though he practised and practised, Remus knew he would never be as good as Oddboy. And the more he practised, the more dispirited he became. People used to think he was a good fiddler, and it was he who would have been asked to play for them if Mr Petamenghi wasn't available. But now they always demanded Oddboy.

One day, while Remus was dutifully doing his daily practice, Grandfather Petamenghi asked Oddboy to harness the horse and cart and go out into the forest to collect logs for the fire. So Oddboy set off to do the old man's bidding. As soon as he'd gone, Remus noticed Oddboy's violin lying on the bed, and he couldn't help picking it up. It didn't seem to be made of the same wood as his, and when he peered inside the body of the instrument, he saw it was painted with oranges and lemons entwined in dark green leaves and encircled with roses – just like the words that had come into his grandfather's head when listening to Oddboy's melody.

Remus put the violin to his chin and drew the bow across the strings. Immediately, the most beautiful sound emerged.

'Oddboy? Is that you?' blind old Mr Petamenghi called out.

Remus hurriedly picked up his own fiddle and scratched the strings. 'No, Grandfather! It's just me, practising,' he answered.

'Hmm . . . For a moment you sounded as good as Oddboy. You're improving,' said his grandfather.

Yes, thought Remus to himself. *If I owned a violin like this, everyone would think I was a wonderful fiddler too.*

The longer Oddboy stayed, the more resentful of him Remus became. It seemed to him that Oddboy was making himself too much at home. Remus began to feel unwanted, and wished that this interloper would go away.

The weather turned very cold. There was snow in the air and the logs were running low. After a while Mr Petamenghi asked Oddboy to take the horse and cart into the forest to collect more wood. Oddboy went to the stable, and as soon as he was out of earshot, Remus said to his grandfather, 'I'll go instead of Oddboy. I know where the best wood is.'

'You're a good lad,' murmured Grandfather Petamenghi.

Oddboy was turning onto the track when Remus ran up and said, 'When you reach the fallen log, take the path to the left, for there you will find plenty of wood.' He knew he was sending Oddboy into a dark, tangled part of the forest where the cart could get mired up, and he might easily get lost.

Expecting Oddboy to be away for a very long time, Remus ran back into the house and, saying not a word, went up to Oddboy's room. There was the violin lying on his bed. He picked it up, put it to his chin and began to play. Strange, beautiful sounds came from the fiddle.

Grandfather Petamenghi called from below. 'Oddboy, come down and play to me in the parlour. I do so love to hear you.'

So Remus went downstairs and, without saying a word, sat near the window playing Oddboy's fiddle. Grandfather listened intently to the notes coming from the strings. 'This is a different sort of music,' he murmured. 'Something's changed. Aren't you happy with us any more? What are you thinking, Oddboy? Play me "The Song of Home".'

But of course it wasn't Oddboy playing, it was Remus, and he couldn't play 'The Song of Home'. The violin wouldn't let him. Instead it was playing out Remus's inner thoughts: by now Oddboy must have reached the log in the wood; he must be following the track to the left, he was thinking. The track ran deep into the forest, where it soon led into a dense thicket and, with the snow falling thick and fast, and the air so cold, Oddboy's fingers would freeze. That notion pleased Remus a lot. If only – oh, if only Oddboy never came back, the marvellous violin would be his for ever, and his grandfather would praise him. That's what Remus was thinking, and those were the thoughts that came from his fingers, speaking through the violin.

His music got faster and faster, and his heart thudded in time to the beat as he thought of the riches he would gain. His grandfather cried out fearfully: 'Oddboy? Is it really you? Your playing disturbs me. I have never heard dark thoughts in your music before. It seems to me full of plotting and scheming; of hatred, even. Where is my grandson? Is he home yet?'

Just then, there was the sound of a horse and cart crunching on the hard snow outside. Oddboy was back. The door was flung open, and there he stood, his arms full of logs. He dumped them in the hearth, then turned and gazed a long and piercing gaze at the deceiving grandson.

'I'm glad you're back so soon, Remus, my boy! Oddboy was playing such disturbing music; it unsettled me.'

'Yes, Grandfather. I'm back with a cart full of logs. I'll stock up the fire and heat up some stew for supper,' said Remus, thrusting the fiddle at Oddboy. What did he care if Oddboy stared at him as if he were a traitor? What could he do about it? How do the dumb speak to the blind? He stomped away defiantly.

Oddboy looked at the blind old man, sprawled in his chair with tears on his cheeks, and began to play 'The Song of Home'.

Grandfather Petamenghi relaxed and smiled. 'That's better,' he sighed. 'Whenever you play that music, I see a beautiful golden land, with groves of orange and lemon trees, and mountains of snow that run down to an azure sea. And I think that must be your home . . . Oddboy . . .' His voice trailed away. 'Is that where you come from?' he murmured, half asleep.

But now Remus became obsessed with driving Oddboy away. He spread stories in the village that there was something definitely odd about Oddboy. 'Our milk curdles whenever Oddboy fetches the pail from the cow; our best hen has stopped laying eggs; chairs move across the room all by themselves; and I saw the kitchen table rise up to the ceiling, all four legs off the ground – I swear! And last week, after Oddboy took out the horse and cart, the horse fell sick.'

Someone murmured, 'A devil's child, to be sure.' Others nodded in agreement.

'Get rid of him, get rid of him,' they muttered. 'We always knew there was something odd about him.'

'But he has cast the biggest spell of all over my grandfather,' said Remus grimly. 'My grandfather thinks he's an angel, not a devil. He won't hear a word said against him. He will never send him away. I think Oddboy has made my grandfather love him more than me.'

'Send him back where he came from,' someone muttered.

'Yes, send him back, send him back . . .' The voices rose in agreement.

'But where *did* he come from?' asked another. Then they all looked up at the mountain.

Through the deep winter, no one did anything. The snow was too thick, and everyone just concentrated on keeping warm and finding enough food to eat.

But one morning, in early spring, some men and boys from the village passed by Mr Petamenghi's cottage in a horse and cart. They said that many of the stone walls had been damaged during the winter, and they were off to the quarry at the base of the mountain to get some more.

'We need the boys to help,' they said.

'Of course,' said Grandfather Petamenghi, and ordered Remus and Oddboy to join the villagers. But very soon into their journey, some of the children began to tease Oddboy.

'You don't belong here – you've brought nothing but bad luck to the village. Did you hear Mrs Borrowday fell and broke her leg? And Mr Heston's dog became sick and died, and Marjorie Yates . . .'

They reached the mountain and set to work collecting stones, all the while telling tales of things that had gone wrong.

'The worst thing,' grumbled Remus, 'is that he's turned my grandfather against me. *I'm* the one who fetches and carries. Don't I do everything for him now that he's blind? But do I get any gratitude? No, it's all Oddboy this, and Oddboy that. He thinks Oddboy can do no wrong. He's ruining my life. We should take him up the mountain. After all, isn't that where he came from?'

'Yes! Let's take him up the mountain,' hissed another boy. 'We might be able to lose him. You wouldn't mind that, would you, Remus?' The lads wandered further away from the main group, and herded Oddboy between them onto a winding path that ascended the mountain. Higher and higher they went, laughing and jeering and shoving Oddboy in the back and tripping him up, as if they hoped he might tumble down the hillside.

At first they were on a track wide enough for a cart, and they barely noticed how the path dwindled. It became narrower and narrower, till there was barely enough room to put one foot in front of the other, and then they realized the danger they were in. The boys stopped and shuddered at the terrifying chasms that yawned below; one false step, and they could plunge to their deaths.

Ahead of them was the thick white mist that never cleared from the upper reaches of the mountain; the mist that no one in the village had ever dared to penetrate; where, perhaps, a magician lived. The boys looked at Oddboy, their gaze full of threat. 'Keep going,' they said, urging him forward into the mist that they themselves wouldn't dare to enter. 'Go home, Oddboy,' they said, blocking his way down.

Oddboy stared at Remus; then, raising an arm in sad farewell, he entered the mist and *disappeared.*

Remus and his friends stood there for a long time, laughing and joking with each other as if to cover their shame, and thinking that Oddboy might reappear any moment; then they could forget that they had thought of doing anything wrong, and go home as if nothing had happened. But all they could hear was the eerie creaking of a glacier, and the occasional trickle of pebbles.

Far below, Remus could see his village bathed in glorious evening sun, and his grandfather's cottage on the edge of the forest. What would he tell him? he wondered. Remus gave one shout – 'Oddboy! We're going back now!' – so that he could honestly say he had tried to find him. There came no answer; only a single shriek from an eagle far above his head.

Shadows were engulfing the slopes like a vast purple cloak, and the boys knew they must get off the mountain before night. 'Just leave him,' they said. 'It's not our fault if he falls over a cliff, or is lost in the mist. Good riddance. He's either in the arms of God or in the lap of the devil.'

And when Remus remembered Oddboy's violin lying on the bed back in the cottage, he shivered to think it could be his now. Soon people would want *him* to be their fiddler, and perhaps it would be like the good old days when it was just him and his grandfather.

'Come on,' Remus said. 'Let's go.'

'You've been away a long time,' cried Mr Petamenghi when Remus came in. 'I was so worried.'

'It was hard work, Grandfather,' cried Remus, his voice light and energetic. 'I'll build up the fire and get supper going.'

'I hope Oddboy didn't damage his fingers shifting all those stones,' sighed the blind old man. 'Let me feel them.' He stretched out his hands.

But Remus said, 'Oddboy is unharnessing the cart and rubbing down the horse.' He couldn't bring himself to tell the truth; his grandfather would be distraught. So, after a while, he opened and shut the door as though Oddboy had come in, and he talked to him as if he were there – 'Oddboy, ladle out three bowls of soup for us!' – and he moved around as if there were two of them.

After supper, Remus clattered the bowls and

spoons, behaving as though Oddboy were at the table. Then, as usual, he helped his grandfather into his chair by the fire, and the old man said, 'Oddboy, play for me.'

Remus's footsteps crossed the room, pretending to be Oddboy. He climbed the stairs and went into the bedroom. There was the wonderful violin lying on the bed. He picked it up and stroked the wood. He took up the bow and tightened the golden hair, then he went downstairs and sat where Oddboy played to the old man each evening.

Remus felt a quiver of excitement as he raised the bow to the strings. He played a single note. It was as pure as a drop of water. He played another note, followed by another and another, shaping it into a tune. He was full of such joy himself that, suddenly, it was Oddboy's tune flowing from the violin.

Grandfather Petamenghi sighed with pleasure, and murmured the words with the music:

'I sing of a land
Where roses blow . . .'

Grandfather Petamenghi had just fallen asleep when Remus heard a tapping at the door.

'Who's there?' he whispered without opening it.

'That's my tune. Give me back my violin.' There was a sudden rustling and flapping of feathers.

'Never,' hissed Remus. 'Go away. I don't know you.' And after a while, the tapping stopped.

The second evening, he again deceived his grandfather, pretending to be himself as well as Oddboy. After supper, when the old man said, 'Play for me, Oddboy,' Remus picked up the fiddle and played. 'What a joy you are to me, Oddboy. Angels couldn't produce such a sound,' he murmured as he fell asleep.

There was a sound of insistent tapping, as if a beak were pecking at the door.

'Who's there?' whispered Remus.

'Give me back my violin.'

'Never,' hissed Remus. 'Go away. You don't belong here.'

On the third night, Remus talked once more as if Oddboy were still around. He made enough sounds for two, and set the table for three, scraping chairs and clattering plates. After he had cleared everything away, his grandfather said, 'Play for me, Oddboy,' and Remus picked up the fiddle and began to play 'The Song of Home'. He hadn't meant to play that tune – he would rather have played something else – but somehow his fingers did whatever they wanted.

Grandfather Petamenghi, who had been relaxed with his head thrown back, leaned forward eagerly, a smile on his face. 'Marvellous, Oddboy! Oh, what a joy you have been to me ever since you came. I hope you will never leave. This is your home now.'

When Remus heard those words, all his jealousy returned. He wanted to shout, 'It's *me* playing, Grandfather. *Me!* See, I play so well now, you don't even know the difference between him and me. And this is not his home!' But he didn't say a word. His feelings rushed into his fingers. The notes became edgy and angry; the music harsh and agitated. A fierce, insistent rhythm took over.

'Stop, Oddboy!' cried Grandfather Petamenghi,

alarmed. 'What's the matter?' But Remus couldn't stop playing.

'Remus, Remus!' the old man called out. 'Has Oddboy been upset by anything today? He's playing differently.'

But there was no reply. The bow bounced on the strings and played even faster; grating, raucous music with an insistent rhythm. Not because Remus wanted it to, but because he no longer had control of his hands, and found he had no voice. Like Oddboy, he had become dumb. His fingers scampered up and down of their own accord, and his foot tapped furiously.

Grandfather Petamenghi wriggled in his chair. 'Oddboy, Oddboy! What's up with you? Calm down – you're making me feel upset.' The old man's feet were tapping uncontrollably.

But no matter how hard Remus tried to play quietly and appease his grandfather, he found he could no longer make the violin do what he wanted, and he couldn't speak.

'I'm too old for this!' panted the old man, who had now leaped from his chair and begun to dance.

He
jigged
and jogged and
bounded
and twirled,

bumping into chairs
and tables. But Remus
couldn't stop. The violin
seemed to be welded
beneath his chin, and his fingers had a mind of their
own. On and on he played, though his arm now
ached and the tips of his fingers began to bleed.

'Stop, I beg you! You'll be the death of me!' cried
the old man, and he grabbed Remus's arm. 'You are
not Oddboy!' he cried in a voice of horror. 'Who

are you? Is it you, Remus? Have you tricked me?' His sightless eyes stared, as if he could force himself to see. 'Stop, stop!'

'He came into our home,' Remus howled through the notes of his violin. 'You think he plays better than I do. You love him more than me. I hate him.' And the bow hit the strings with such savagery that his grandfather whirled around and fell to the floor.

Remus was horrified. Had he killed him? He opened his mouth to cry, 'Grandfather! I'm sorry, I'm sorry,' but no sound came out, and anyway, it was too late to be sorry. He wanted to fall on his knees and beg forgiveness, but the violin wouldn't let him.

Then there came such a tapping, pecking, knocking and banging all around the house, and such a beating at the doors and windows, and a voice cried out, 'Give me back my fiddle.'

The door sprang open in a flurry of snow and feathers and, unable to prevent himself, Remus danced through into the cold, cold night. Behind him lay his grandfather. Remus was sure he was dying, and he desperately wanted to turn back. But he couldn't; and with his fingers scampering up and down the strings uncontrollably, he danced away.

He danced into the dark forest, stumbling and tripping, but his fingers never ceased playing. All through the night he danced and fiddled, and the next day too. Day after day, night after night, he fiddled, and wondered if he must fiddle till he dropped down dead. His feet carried him to a rushing river, and joyfully, he thought, *If I can dunk myself in the river, perhaps the water will drown the fiddle for ever and free me from this curse.* 'River, river, drown my fiddle,' he cried out in his innermost soul.

But though he went in up to his neck, the fish in the river leaped and mocked him: 'Fiddle away, fiddle away. We don't want you,' and he danced out again.

Another day, Remus saw some charcoal burners stoking up a fire, and for a while the fiddle danced him up to the flames. 'Fire, fire, burn my fiddle,' his soul wept and pleaded.

But the fire seemed to taunt him. It sizzled and fizzled as if ice had been thrown on it; it spat and crackled and turned blue and orange, but it wouldn't burn him or his fiddle. 'Go away, go away!' the flames shrieked. 'You're no use to us. You can be no fuel for this fire.' And not one hair of his head was singed and his violin wasn't even scorched by the heat.

'Go away,' shouted the charcoal burners, certain they had seen the devil himself.

After dancing through another day and night, Remus came across a church where a gravedigger was turning over the earth in a freshly dug grave. Would he find mercy here? he wondered. The fiddle carried him right to the edge of a deep, deep grave, where they had just laid the coffin. Perhaps it was a grave for his grandfather. Full of remorse for all he'd done, he longed to throw himself in. *If only the gravedigger could bury me and this accursed fiddle, then surely I'd find peace at last*, he thought.

Dancing to the very edge, Remus toppled into the grave. But even though the gravedigger shovelled and shovelled, the earth flew out again, as if it too were dancing, and out leaped Remus, fiddling for all he was worth. The gravedigger ran away, howling in terror, thinking the corpse must be a wild and unrepentant spirit.

'*Ahhh!*' shrieked Remus with his whole being. 'What kind of fiddle is this? The river won't drown it, the fire won't burn it, and the earth won't bury it. I'm not wanted by God or the devil himself. Who can save me?' And still he danced on.

Another dawn was breaking, and suddenly, as he passed a wide-spreading yew tree, he heard a mumbling. An old man lay huddled at its base, murmuring in his sleep. 'It's all my fault,' he moaned. 'Why did I take in that odd boy? Why did I let that violin enchant me, and make me think that music was more important than my own flesh and blood? Now I've lost both of them. Oh Remus, dear boy, will I ever find you?'

'Grandfather, Grandfather!' How Remus tried to shout, to scream, to call out. 'I'm here, alive! You're alive! I'm sorry, I'm sorry.' But no sound left his throat and he couldn't stop dancing. Then, suddenly, the violin was playing the melody his grandfather loved so much. Remus hadn't meant to play it, but the violin made him, and even as he danced away, the old man, with sightless eyes, sat up, murmuring the words to the tune he could hear:

'I sing of a land
Where roses blow,

And lemons grow,
And orange trees float in a deep green shade.'

And with a broken-hearted voice, Grandfather Petamenghi cried out, 'Oddboy! Give me back my grandson!'

It was then that Remus looked up towards the mountain and saw a great bird wheeling around in the sky. 'You can have your fiddle back, Oddboy,' he whispered through his battered fingers. 'Take it.'

Immediately, his feet led him to the mountain. Higher and higher and higher he jogged, along the trail where he and the village boys had driven Oddboy; skimming the edges of precipices, along thin paths fit only for tiny hooves, springing from rock to rock like a mountain goat; and still his fingers flew up and down, and the bow clawed at the strings, producing the wildest of sounds.

Remus came to the edge of the mist, as he knew he would, and entered its wafting coils. Even the roar of a cataract couldn't drown out his frantic playing. He danced towards the boiling waterfall, thinking, *Now is my end.* But there in the greyness, perched like a bird on a rock jutting out over the waterfall, with spray flinging all around him, was a figure. It was Oddboy.

Remus stopped; his fingers stopped. His bowing arm dropped to his side, and the violin hung loose in his hand. The playing and dancing had ceased.

He stood on the edge with the river churning below, and held out the violin. He felt words rushing up his throat: *I'm sorry for what I did to you. I'm sorry I took your violin.* The boy didn't move. Then, because he wanted to, Remus lifted the violin back to his chin and raised the bow. He began to play, 'The Song of Home'.

Oddboy got to his feet and turned towards Remus. He spoke in a foreign tongue, yet Remus understood. 'I only wanted to join in. I used to listen to you from up here and wished I belonged down there with all of you.' In a sudden movement, he snatched away the violin and, with a great cry, flung it, spinning, into the spray of the waterfall.

There was a mighty *crack*, like a tree being struck by lightning, and the magician appeared, as huge as the evening shadows beginning to envelop the mountain. 'Is this how you repay me for the wonderful gift I gave you?' he roared and, throwing his arms wide, uttered a dreadful incantation. Oddboy teetered to the edge of the plunging waterfall and fell, down, down, down, twirling and whirling like a falling leaf. He spun as if caught in a vortex, and vanished into the watery mist of the pool churning below. The magician looked at Remus and stretched out a long-fingered hand. 'Come.'

Remus staggered backwards, away from the waterfall, away from the magician. But just as he felt himself surrendering to the spell, an amazing bird hurtled upwards through the spray; a bird with green and yellow plumage, and blue under-feathers, and a white breast that glistened like snow. It flew into the magician's face, beating its wings and plucking at his eyes.

'Away, away!' it cried. 'Away, away!' It flapped and pecked, while Remus threw himself out of the curtain of mist and back to the other side. As he scrambled and slithered down the mountain, eyes fixed on his home below, he heard the cry, 'Away, away!' and saw the bird rising free above the mountain and then turning towards the south.

The villagers were preparing for the May Day celebrations and the arrival of summer. No one ever spoke of Oddboy again. It was as though he had never come among them. And, besides, what need had they these days for anyone other than Remus, who played even better than his grandfather ever had?

But when the trees had burst into leaf, and hedgerows glistened with hawthorn, and violets strewed the paths, Remus played, the villagers danced, and old blind Grandfather Petamenghi listened with a contented smile on his face. And from out of an azure sky came a bird with green and yellow plumage the colour of oranges and lemons, with sky-blue underfeathers, and a breast of snowy white. The old man couldn't see it, but he tipped his head skywards, humming under his breath as it warbled, 'I sing of a land where roses blow,' and he remembered.

THE NIGHT PRINCESS

A gift is not always welcome, and not all wishes can be fulfilled. Beware the desire that may require a sacrifice.

When the Queen of the Night knew she was going to have a baby, she whispered to her husband, the king: 'I wish for a daughter whose skin is as dark as night, whose eyes are as silver as stars, and whose hair is as curly black as storm clouds.'

In due course, the baby was born, and she was exactly as her mother desired, so they named her 'Desire'. They held such a party up there in the night skies, and everyone from the Night Kingdom was invited: star maidens and comet princes, night fairies and shooting-star warriors. And all the night creatures from the earth below were invited too:

cats and bats, and foxes and badgers, and nightjars and owls;

all spangled and bangled, and glimmering and shimmering, and glinting with jet and coal and iron, all went to the party to celebrate the birth of Princess Desire.

And what a party it was. Each guest brought the little baby a present: the nightingale gave her a beautiful voice, the fox gave her cunning, the owl gave her wisdom, the night flower gave her fragrance, and others bestowed goodness, happiness, compassion, courage and a long, long life.

At last it was the turn of the oldest night fairy; she was a grandmother comet who roamed the universe and only made an appearance every one hundred and fifty years. Everyone was happy that she could attend. They saw her zooming through the night sky with her fiery tail, arriving just in time for Desire's party. The Night Queen was thrilled, and hoped that the grandmother's gift would be very special.

Grandmother Comet bent over the star-spangled crib and murmured, 'Oh beauteous child, to you I give the gift of sacrifice,' and three drops of blood fell from her finger onto the sleeping child.

Those present pondered the strangeness of this offering. They knew it would be stronger than any of the other gifts – but what did it mean?

Now someone else in the universe was watching. It was the Sun King. He was furious that he hadn't been invited. He threw his eclipse cloak over his great shining body, and decided to attend anyway. This vast dark-cloaked figure arrived at the palace and demanded entry. The star night watchmen quaked with fear and gave way. He was led into the banqueting hall and stood before the King and Queen of the Night, glowering and terrifying beneath his shadowy cloak.

'I think you forgot to invite me!' His voice crackled like a forest fire.

Everyone shrank away, as a terrible burning heat emanated from him.

'We beg your most humble pardon, kind sir,' said the Night King. 'Please forgive our oversight, but I fear it is because we do not know you.'

'Oh yes,' sizzled the Sun King. 'You know me all right. Am I not the Giver of Life? Am I not the Ruler of the Universe?' He came before the infant's cradle. 'Nonetheless I have brought a gift for the Night Princess. It is the gift of fire.'

He drew out a burning brand of flame from

under his cloak. Screams echoed around the heavens as, before the horrified guests, the Sun King tossed the brand high into the air above the cot.

Then he vanished in a blaze of light. Everyone cringed in terror, blinded and scorched. The flaming brand was about to plunge downwards onto the baby, when Grandmother Comet immediately flung herself over Desire with open mouth and swallowed it.

'Thank you, thank you!' The Night Queen wept as she realized how she had nearly lost her beloved child.

'You may thank me now,' said Grandmother Comet, her voice bubbling like an undersea volcano, 'but I warn you: if one single ray of sun ever touches Princess Desire, she will be burned to ashes. Guard her well.' Then she sprang upwards and continued on her long orbit, her burning tail stretching for thousands of miles behind her.

Year by year, the little girl grew up, and the whole universe knew that she was brighter and more beautiful than any star in the firmament.

Every night she was to be seen galloping along the

Milky Way

on
her black
mare, Midnight,
racing the wind demons.

Never far behind was her groom,
Dark. It was his duty to protect the princess
and make sure she returned safely to the palace
before even the thinnest crack of dawn. But the
princess was a difficult person to keep up with. She
was always so full of curiosity, so daring, playing
tricks and sometimes hiding from him. Worst of all,
Princess Desire wanted to see the whole world from
the ground instead of from the sky. She courted
danger by coming down to earth. Every night she
rode out on her horse, and landed in a different

place; she roamed deserts and jungles and meadows and mountains. She went trotting through silent sleeping villages, through vast cities of towering skyscrapers and office blocks, of domes and steeples and minarets, where the lights never dimmed; lights which, it seemed to her, were even more marvellous than the stars in the firmament.

Dark was nervous and would say, 'Princess, Princess, we shouldn't come here; the lights of the city might deceive us; here, we may not distinguish night from day – we might be caught out by the coming of dawn.'

But secretly, Desire longed to see the world by daylight.

She discovered that people worshipped the sun: they built temples to him, drew pictures and carved statues to him. So great and all powerful was the sun; he was nameless, but people called him Ra, Surya, Helios, Khepri, Oriana or Khorshid. There were names for his rays at dawn, for making the skies and the oceans blue by noon, and names for his golden, purple and orange colours as he faded at evening. She saw great standing stones arranged so that the sun would rise through the arch of one, and descend through the arch of another; the altars of churches always faced east, where the sun rose, and imams in their mosques climbed up high, towering minarets so that they could always see the first rays of the sun in the morning, and the last rays at night. She heard songs and hymns and prayers to the sun; music and dance were devoted to him for every time of day. All life came from the sun, and some said that he was God himself. More and more, Desire longed to see this glorious celestial body; to see it rise and set. But, with a sigh, she accepted her parents' rule that on no account must she ever let one ray of sunlight fall upon her.

One night, as she and Dark were galloping across the heavens, she noticed a light bobbing in the darkness somewhere below on earth. 'What's that?' she asked Dark.

'Just some human carrying a lamp,' he replied.

'Let's go and see,' cried Desire, and turned her horse earthwards.

The land was strangely bright, but not from sunlight – otherwise Dark would never have let her descend. No, the land was covered in shining snow, and struggling through the drifts was a young farmer holding a lamp, hurrying to attend to one of his ewes, which was about to give birth. All night long, he protected the ewe with his cloak, and soothed her as tenderly as a mother would her child – until at last, a slippery, leggy, wobbly lamb slid out into the world.

Its high-pitched bleats rang through the sky.

When Desire saw how devotedly the farmer looked after the mother and her offspring, she fell in love with him. Each night she descended to earth and followed him across the fields to tend to his flock, and later, as he stumbled home and fell into bed. Each night, Desire dismounted and crept up to a window to watch him. Never had she believed such a man could exist: his body was as pale as dawn, his hair as golden as the rays of the sun, his long limbs flowed from him like rivers, and she called him Day, and thought that she could bear never to see the sun or the light of day so long as she could be with this farmer.

All night long she hung in the ivy and honeysuckle that grew up the walls; all night long she pressed her face to the window, just gazing upon him, till Dark cried, 'My lady, we must go. The night is fading. We must leave now before the rays of the sun pierce the sky.'

Reluctantly, Princess Desire would mount her jet-black steed and gallop back into the night, her heart full of love for the farmer.

Night after night she came down to earth and returned to the farm.

She watched the man sleeping,

dreaming, or waking to attend to his animals when they needed him. She peered secretly, midnight-blue, through the leaves of oak trees, and sprinkled dew across the fields like diamonds. Then one night, as Day bent over a ewe, helping with the birth, two burning green eyes gazed at him through the darkness. A wolf, muscles taut, body poised, crouched low among the trees, ready to pounce on the shepherd and his sheep. Desire saw the danger, and immediately flung her night cloak over the farmer so that he vanished from the sight of the wolf.

The wolf's howl of bewildered rage echoed around the hills.

Desire enveloped the farmer for the rest of the night until Dark told her that it was time to leave.

She gazed tenderly at her sleeping mortal. 'But it's still night. What if the wolf returns?' she whispered.

'I'll stay on guard until daybreak, my lady,' Dark assured her. 'The sunlight can't hurt me. But promise me you will ride immediately to the Night Palace, and not look back.'

'Dear, faithful Dark, I promise. And promise me you won't let any harm come to this man.'

'I promise,' Dark replied, though in his heart he wished the princess loved him as much as she loved this simple farmer.

When the first shafts of light broke through the curtain of the night, Dark unfurled the night cloak from the sleeping farmer and, like a purple mist, rose upwards from the dewy fields. In the distance, he saw a young woman hurrying down the lane with a dog running alongside her. Dark hovered over the fields, watching as she flew across the meadow with a cry: 'Dearest love, my darling! Oh my goodness! Are you hurt?' And she threw herself down beside the farmer, covering his face with kisses.

The farmer sat up and gathered the maiden into his arms, shuddering. 'I had such a strange dream; at least, I *think* it was a dream,' he murmured. 'I was about to be torn to pieces by a wolf, when out of the darkness came a shape – a beauteous woman with a face as black as night. Her eyes gleamed into mine like stars. She took my head in her lap and covered me with a cloak of invisibility. She saved my life.'

'Sweetheart mine,' murmured the young woman, holding him close. 'Thank goodness we are soon to be married, and I can work alongside you and protect you.'

When Dark returned to the Night Palace, the princess was waiting keenly to hear more about the farmer. 'Is Day safe?' she asked quietly.

'Safe, my lady,' he replied, then gently told her

about the maiden who was soon to marry the farmer she had saved. How Dark's heart ached when he saw the pain in her eyes; the longing and the love she now felt.

'I must see him again,' she wept. 'Perhaps if he saw me, he would love me and come to our palace in the night sky?'

The next night, Desire galloped down to earth, to the farmer's house.

Now that all his lambs were born, Day's routine had returned to waking with the sun. By night he simply slept, his head thrown back with exhaustion, a faint smile around his lips as dreams flitted across his brow, and Desire would stare at him through the window.

One summer's night it was so hot that he left his window open, and Desire slipped over the sill and hovered by his bed, just gazing upon him with love. His pale, bare feet hung over the end of the bed, and she couldn't resist tickling them, for she longed to wake him.

And wake he did, with a start, sitting bolt upright, suddenly aware that there was a presence in his room. There, laughing at him from the foot of his bed, was the most beautiful creature he had ever laid eyes on. 'It's you!' he exclaimed with sudden recognition. 'I thought you were a dream. Who are you?'

'I am Princess Desire, daughter of the King of the Night,' she said.

'It was you who saved me from the wolf?' asked the farmer incredulously.

She nodded.

'Where do you come from?'

'From the firmament, from the stars, from everlasting night,' she cried.

He looked confused, as though he couldn't imagine such a place.

'My horse is outside. Come, ride with me and let me show you where I live!'

Her black mare pawed at the window, and Desire pulled the farmer onto Midnight's back and sprang up before him, clutching the reins. 'Go!' she cried, patting her horse's head, her voice tinkling like scattering diamonds. 'Go!' And Midnight leaped into the sky and galloped towards the moon, with Dark following sadly after, terrified of the tragedy that might befall his beloved princess for loving a mortal.

She galloped with her farmer, Day, across the night skies, dodging falling stars and the debris of exploding universes; they swam in pools of moonlight, and sang with nightingales; they explored all the nightscapes of the earth and even the inky depths of the oceans.

'I love you, Princess of the Night. I want you to be my wife.'

'And I have loved you ever since I saw you,' she replied. 'Why don't you come and be my husband and live with me in the night skies? And we will have the entire firmament at our disposal; I can show you the whole world and its glories, if you will come with me.'

The farmer felt a glow of love and excitement such as he had never before experienced, and when they returned before dawn, he begged her to come again.

'I will, I will!' she exclaimed happily.

When Dark heard this, he knew he must report back to the king and queen. With a sad heart, he went before them and told of Princess Desire's love for a mortal. 'He is a creature of the day,' said Dark, 'and though he often works at night, he is a servant of the sun.'

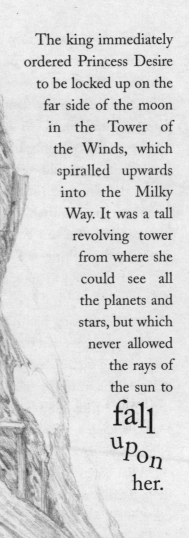

The king immediately
ordered Princess Desire
to be locked up on the
far side of the moon
in the Tower of
the Winds, which
spiralled upwards
into the Milky
Way. It was a tall
revolving tower
from where she
could see all
the planets and
stars, but which
never allowed
the rays of
the sun to
fall
upon
her.

'It's for your own safety, my dear,' her father told her. 'You must stay here until we have found you a suitable husband.'

The princess had servants and friends to keep her company, and music to delight the ear, and any number of amusements, but all these meant nothing to her and she could only think of her farmer, for whom she pined pitifully.

Every now and then, the king and queen visited and told her of a suitor who wanted to marry her. But each time, Princess Desire shook her head and found excuses not to accept him.

Now, the Sun King had not failed to notice what a beautiful princess this baby had grown up to be. So beautiful, in fact, that he thought she was the only being in the universe suitable to be a bride for his son, Prince Fire. He sent a message that he wished for an audience with the King and Queen of the Night as he had a proposition to make.

'What could it be?' they wondered, and couldn't help feeling it had something to do with their daughter.

They sat side by side on their silver thrones

waiting for the Sun King's arrival.

They heard a fanfare of trumpets – a sound that shimmered through the palace with a blinding light – and suddenly, a vast, cloaked figure strode into the throne room. As before, the Sun King was enveloped in a black cloak so as not to set fire to the Night Kingdom. They indicated a throne of stars for their royal visitor to be seated, and for some moments there was silence as they all contemplated each other.

At last the Sun King spoke. 'We have noted the way in which Princess Desire has grown into a woman of incomparable beauty and goodness of heart. We regret our anger at her birth and our offence taken at not being invited to her party. We wish to create friendly bonds between our two kingdoms, and I therefore request the hand in marriage of your daughter to my son, Prince Fire. In this way, the curse will be lifted from her, and she will no longer be endangered by any beam of sunlight, no matter how weak or how strong.'

The Night King and Queen looked at each other. It seemed to them to be an eminently reasonable proposal; anything that restored the friendship between the Sun and the Moon had to be a good thing. They promised to talk it over with their daughter and let the Sun King know as soon as possible.

How Princess Desire's heart ached. She knew how much she would please her parents if only she would accept Prince Fire as a husband. And wasn't she tempted when she thought of what freedom she would gain from having the terrible spell lifted; the spell which meant she would be destroyed if one single glimmer of sunlight ever fell upon her? Wouldn't she have the power to roam the firmament by night and by day? Wouldn't she be able to see all the colours of daylight: the green of grass and trees, the pinks, purples, blues, reds and yellows of flowers and birds; indeed the colours of the rainbow? But all she could think about was how much she loved the human farmer, Day, down below on earth, and suddenly, none of those things seemed as important as her love for him.

So Desire wept as she told her parents that she couldn't, indeed wouldn't, accept Prince Fire as a husband.

'Then I fear, that you must continue to remain

in this tower until you agree,' they told her, and swept away in anger and distress.

King and Queen Night summoned Dark, their daughter's faithful guardian. 'Talk to her. You are her best friend – she may listen to you. Make her see sense. Remind her of her duties to us and to her kingdom.'

So Dark was taken up the spiral of winds to the tower and admitted into the princess's chambers.

'Have you come to help me? Have you come to take me away? Dear Dark, my best and only friend?' she cried.

'My lady,' whispered Dark. 'Love is so thoughtless. It doesn't care whether or not it can be fulfilled. Some love has to stay secret, unfulfilled, unrequited. No one can tell you not to love this mortal; only you can step back with that love still in your heart, and give him up to the human woman who can be his wife in a way that you can't. If he married you, he would be condemned never again to see the light of day. If you married him, you know that one glimmer of sunlight upon you would destroy you. This love cannot be. I cannot ask you to forget him, but I can remind you of your duty to your parents and to the kingdom. Bid him farewell, dear Princess, and let us now leave him for ever.'

Princess Desire looked at him as if he had betrayed her; as if he could no longer be counted as her friend and most loyal bodyguard. And Dark's heart felt as though it were breaking when she ordered him away. 'After all,' she raged, 'I am being asked to marry the son of a king who cursed me in the most dreadful way. How could I ever trust him or his son? I would be a wife, yet nothing more than a prisoner.'

So Dark had to return to the Night Kingdom and report back that he had failed to persuade the princess.

'Then she must stay in the tower. It's for her own good,' answered the king sternly.

When the Sun King heard that Princess Desire had refused his son in marriage, he was furious. He raged over the universe; his heat beat down pitilessly on the poor earth below; the lakes and rivers began to dry up, thirsty people searched desperately for water, while birds fluttered help-lessly in the leafless trees. Worst of all, farmers could no longer grow crops on their parched lands, and their animals were dying.

The farmer, whom the princess loved so desperately, worked night and day trying to save his flock.

Once more, Dark came to the tower and told the horrified princess what was happening. 'The earth is dying, my lady. Your own beloved farmer will die too. Only you can save them.'

'Dear Dark, this is my last request: let me see my farmer for one last time and then, I promise, no more.'

After much anguished thought, Dark agreed. Secretly, he went to the starry stables, and led forth Midnight, the princess's mare. He rode her up until he reached the top of the tower, and there she neighed at the window.

The princess rushed forward with joy and amazement. 'Oh Dark, dear Dark, thank you, thank you! I should never have doubted your loyalty and love for me.'

'Please, Princess,' he cried. 'Let this be your last visit to the mortal. Say your farewell to him.

You and he can never be married. Let him go with his chosen maiden. Wish him happiness.'

'Don't spoil my pleasure!' exclaimed Desire, climbing through the tower window and leaping onto her horse. 'Come on, let's go!' And she galloped down towards the parched earth and the farmer's cottage, followed by her faithful Dark.

Once again, she hovered in the now shrivelled honeysuckle outside the farmer's window. There he lay, restlessly tossing with anxiety, for he was soon to be married and he dreaded what the future might bring.

The Night Princess slid over the windowsill and, once again, stood at the foot of his bed and stroked his bare feet. As before, he awoke, and saw her with joy. Then tears rolled down his cheeks. 'Beloved Princess,' he wept. 'As you didn't come for so long, I thought you no longer loved me. In any case, I knew I couldn't live with you. Who would care for the farm and my sheep if I left to live with you in the Night Kingdom? What's more, I am betrothed to a sweet maid, and am to be married. I could not betray her. But now the earth is dying and I don't know what is to become of us.'

'If you will come with me for one last ride,' replied Desire, 'I shall never trouble you again, and this earth will recover and your farm will thrive; I promise you.'

Joyfully, filled with hope, yet also immeasurable sadness, Day rose from his bed and climbed through the window onto Midnight's back.

Instead of taking the reins herself, the Night Princess mounted behind him. 'You lead the way. Why don't you show me one thing which gives you joy on this earth that you tread as a mortal? Take the reins and ride there with me for this one last time.'

So the farmer took up the reins, gave a gentle dig into Midnight's flanks, and they rose up into the starry sky.

He was exhilarated. 'There's one thing I've always wanted to see, and I know it would give you the greatest pleasure too. Let this be my gift to you; one we shall both remember for ever.'

'Yes, yes! Where are we going?' asked the princess, weeping quietly.

'That's my secret,' said Day. 'I want it to be a surprise.'

'On the way to our destination, let me see the earth by your light,' he cried. So she showed him the Taj Mahal, and the Great Wall of China, snaking away in the moonlight, gleaming dark like a vast serpent. He saw the Alps and the Himalayas, majestic in midnight snow, and the whitest and sweetest of scented flowers that only opened by night.

'Now I will show you the one thing above all others that lifts up my heart and makes me glad to be alive,' he shouted, and turned Midnight's head towards the east.

farmer galloped over the face of the earth.

'Madam, madam!' Dark galloped up alongside his mistress with alarm. 'Turn back. Return to the tower. It is nearly dawn.'

'I can't turn back now!' she shouted. 'I must see the one thing my beloved most adores on this earth.' And pressing her face into the farmer's back, she dug her heels into Midnight's flanks, and urged her onwards.

'Where are you going?' Dark yelled as, instead of riding skywards towards the moon, they galloped on across the face of the earth.

'Go back, Dark! Tell my father and mother that

I love a mortal and can never marry another. I beg forgiveness. Go back!'

Dark tried to catch up with her. How could he ever go back without his mistress? He would rather die. But he lost them amongst the racing clouds, and thought he glimpsed them riding down towards a forest below. He followed. 'Your highness! Princess!' he called out desperately, as they plunged into the trees.

At first he thought he saw shreds of silver light caught among the branches and brambly paths, reflected in woodland pools or running streams, but when he raced towards them, they vanished. As the night went on, Dark began to feel a terror in his bones. Where was the princess? It would soon be dawn. She knew the penalty of being out in even the first glimmer of day. He called again, desperately, begging her to let him take her home. But no answering voice came; only the flutter of disturbed birds, and the scuffling of foxes.

Having lost Dark in the forest, Desire urged her farmer upwards again. 'Are we far from your destination?' she called.

'Not far, not far!' he replied. They broke out of the forest canopy, and finally, ahead, they saw a vast black space where land and sky were indivisible.

'There!' he cried, pointing to earth. 'This is what I was looking for.'

Princess Night saw, by the light of a brilliant moon, a vast plain with a ring of standing stones; huge upright stones capped with lintels like open doors that led into a celestial mansion; giant dancers who would turn, revolve and leap in celebration of life and death.

The farmer brought the horse down and landed in the centre of the circle. He helped Princess Desire dismount. 'Of all the magnificent creations of the world, my love, this is the most extraordinary. I thought I would die and never see it. But you have made it possible. Let us wait here, you and I, and remember this moment for ever. Then we can part and live our lives knowing that we have created our own eternity.'

He folded his arms around her and, turning her face to look through the broadest stone doorway to the eastern horizon, murmured into her hair, 'Watch the sky and wait.'

She gazed up at the full moon. It was beginning to wane. She knew what Day was waiting for. Her eyes scanned her kingdom, where the stars flickered, weaker. Desire leaned into his embrace, pressed her black night's cheek against his, felt the life in his body rushing through his veins, and began to sing a song of farewell.

Dark galloped frantically through the sky, searching for his beloved mistress. Any moment now, the eggshell fabric of the heavens would break, and release the rays of the sun. Then he heard her song and saw them. He plunged downwards into the stone circle just as a thin shaft of pale pink light slid through a crack in the sky above. He flung himself off his horse and raced towards the lovers, standing in the Gateway to the Rising Sun. Even as he enveloped the princess in his night cloak, he knew he was too late. But still, he dragged her out of the fatal doorway, thrusting the farmer away. Within his desperate embrace, Dark felt a burning heat which he knew would destroy them both.

A burst of flame seared high into the skies, then broke up into a million specks of stardust as, all day long, the vengeful Sun King rampaged across the skies in his rage, bringing havoc to the world below. But as evening approached, and with his fury spent, he gazed down at the temple of stones built to honour him as well as the moon. He saw beyond the broad doorway facing towards the east a stone, separate from the rest; a leaning stone, reaching inwards towards the circle, as if trying to see the rising sun and yet escape its rays. Here, the mortal, Day, knelt weeping silently, his arms embracing the stone. At last, the Sun King felt pity, and marvelled at the love of the Night Princess for her mortal. With his ebbing rays, he enveloped the farmer and bore him home.

As the sun set and the day finally darkened, the Night King and his queen rode out frantically in their chariot to find out where their daughter was. A trail of stardust and sparks from a horse's hooves led them to the great plain. Dismounting, they wandered among the giant stones, and there they saw the leaning stone, and realized with awe their daughter's fate.

Another stone lay fallen near by. At last the Night King and Queen understood. Of all the gifts the princess had been given on the occasion of her birth – courage, beauty, justice and love – she had finally used her last: sacrifice. And with Dark's sacrifice in trying to save her, the farmer and the earth were spared and life could go on.

It was the day of his wedding, and the farmer awoke just before sunrise. There was a strange pre-dawn light in the room, and a sound sweeter than any music he had ever heard: it was raining. He leaned out of his window. The smell of honeysuckle overwhelmed him as he looked up into the fading night sky.

Twinkling high above was a star he fancied he had never noticed before. As it dimmed, he was overwhelmed with a sense of loss.

But then the sun burst through, turning the raindrops into a million rainbows. The farmer smiled and turned away, ready to greet his new bride.

ACKNOWLEDGEMENTS

I was so fortunate in having Kirsten Armstrong as my meticulous and supportive editor who ensured the stories in *Blackberry Blue* were as good as could be, and I thank Richard Collingridge for his eerie, romantic and evocative illustrations. Also much appreciation to Dominica Clements and Clair Lansley for their creative designs and layouts. Finally, I thank my sister, Romie who, with her excellent eye and ear gave me such useful feedback.

ABOUT THE AUTHOR

Jamila Gavin's first book, *The Magic Orange Tree*, was published in 1979 and she has since been writing steadily, producing critically acclaimed novels and collections of short stories.

She has been shortlisted for many of the major children's book awards, including the Smarties Award and the Guardian Children's Fiction Award. *Coram Boy* won the Children's Whitbread Award and was shortlisted for the Carnegie Medal, before being adapted for the stage. *The Wheel of Surya*, part one of the *Surya* trilogy, was runner-up for the Guardian Award, and the other two titles were also shortlisted.

ABOUT THE ILLUSTRATOR

Richard Collingridge was born in Hammersmith, London. He studied Illustration and graduated with Honours in 2008. His debut picture book, *When It Snows*, was published to great critical acclaim and was shortlisted for the V&A Illustration Award.